"What happened?"
Daniel asked gently

Tears clogged her throat. This was the first time anyone had asked her about the past; the first time anyone had guessed there was more to her desire to live so quietly than merely a love of the Avon countryside.

She wanted to tell him, and yet she was afraid to. Why? In case he dismissed her fears as foolish as her parents had done? In case he was embarrassed by them as her London friends had been? Or just in case he simply did not understand the trauma of what she'd endured and how it had affected her.

And then he smiled at her, and in the warmth of his eyes she saw a promise that dazzled and awed her.

PENNY JORDAN was constantly in trouble in school because of her inability to stop daydreaming—especially during French lessons. In her teens she was an avid romance reader, although it didn't occur to her to try writing one herself until she was older. "My first half-dozen attempts ended up ingloriously," she remembers, "but I persevered, and one manuscript was finished." She plucked up the courage to send it to a publisher, convinced her book would be rejected. It wasn't, and the rest is history! Penny is married and lives in Cheshire.

Penny Jordan continues to make history. *Silver*, the second mainstream novel from the *New York Times* bestselling author of *Power Play*, was published in October.

Books by Penny Jordan

Don't miss any of our special offers. Write to us at the following address for information on our newest releases.

Harlequin Reader Service
P.O. Box 1397, Buffalo, NY 14240
Canadian address: P.O. Box 603,
Fort Erie, Ont. L2A 5X3

PENNY JORDAN

time for trust

Harlequin Books

TORONTO • NEW YORK • LONDON
AMSTERDAM • PARIS • SYDNEY • HAMBURG
STOCKHOLM • ATHENS • TOKYO • MILAN

Harlequin Presents first edition February 1991
ISBN 0-373-11339-0

Original hardcover edition published in 1990
by Mills & Boon Limited

TIME FOR TRUST

CHAPTER ONE

JESSICA heard the grandfather clock striking eleven. She lifted her head from her work, her concentration broken. The grandfather clock had been acquired through the ancient custom of exchange and barter still very definitely alive in this quiet part of the Avon countryside.

At first she had been very pleased with her 'payment' for one of her larger tapestries; she had even continued to be pleased when the thing had virtually had to be dismantled in order to be installed in the small hallway of her stone cottage, and had then required the services of an extremely expensive and highly individualistic clock mender.

In fact, it was only when she realised what the clock was going to mean in terms of interruptions to her concentration on her work that she began to doubt the wisdom of owning it.

Mind you, she allowed fair-mindedly, it did have its advantages. For instance today, if it had not interrupted her, she would doubtless have worked on until it was far too late to go to the post office. Today, Wednesday, was half-day closing, and she had a tapestry finished and ready to post to the exclusive shop in Bath which sold her work for her.

She had always loved embroidery from being quite small. She remembered how amused and then

5

irritated her parents had been with her interest in it.

Her interest in tapestry had come later, when she knew more about her subject. She had spent a wonderful summer training at the Royal School of Needlework which had confirmed her conviction that her love of the craft meant that she wanted it to be far more than merely a hobby.

Now, five years after that fateful summer, she spent her time either working for the National Trust on the conservation and repair of their tapestries or designing and making tapestries of her own—some for sale through the shop in Bath, and others on direct commissions from people who had seen her work and fallen in love with it.

The tapestry she was working on today was one such commission. Her workroom at the top of her small cottage had a large window to let in the light she needed for her work. It overlooked the countryside to the rear of the small row of cottages of which hers was one. This view had inspired many of her designs; every day it changed, sometimes subtly, sometimes dramatically, and she knew she would never tire of looking at it.

She loved this part of the country with its quiet peace—just as she loved the solitude of her work and life-style. Both made her feel secure...safe... And those were feelings she needed desperately.

She shivered a little. How long was it going to be before she succeeded in wiping her memory free of the past? How long was it going to be before she woke up in the morning without that clutching, panicky feeling of sick fear tensing her body?

She still had nightmares about it ... Still remembered every vivid detail of that appalling day.

It had started so normally—getting up, leaving her parents' fashionable London house for work. Her father was the chairman of the élite merchant bank which had been founded one hundred and fifty years previously by his ancestor.

All her life, Jessica had been conscious of her parents' disappointment that their only child should be a daughter. Nothing was ever said, but all the time she was at school, being encouraged to work hard, to get good results, she had known of her parents' real feelings. She ought to have been a boy; a boy to follow in her father's footsteps, to head the bank and follow tradition. But she wasn't—she was a girl ...

Every time she heard her father say that it made no difference, that these days women were equally as capable as men, that there was no reason at all why she should not eventually take his place, she had sensed his real feelings—had known that she must work doubly hard at school, that she must do everything she could to make up to her parents for the disappointment of her sex.

She had known from being quite young what fate held in store for her. She would go to university, get a degree and then join her father in the bank, where she would be trained for the important role that would one day be hers.

'And, of course, it isn't the end of the world,' she had once heard her father saying to her mother. 'One day she'll marry, and then there'll be grandsons ...'

But by the time she left university with her degree, she had known that she didn't want to make a career in banking.

Every time she'd walked into the imposing Victorian edifice that housed the bank she had felt as though a heavy weight descended on her shoulders, as though something inside her was slowly dying.

Her father's plan was that she would follow in his footsteps, learning their business from the bottom rung, slowly making her way up the ladder, moving from department to department.

Everyone had been kind to her, but she had felt suffocated by the weight of her responsibility, by the bank itself and its solidity. Whenever she could she escaped to Avon to stay with her godmother, an old schoolfriend of her mother's.

She knew that she was disappointing her parents—that they could not understand the *malaise* that affected her.

And then came the event that was to have such a cataclysmic effect on her life...

Warningly, the clock chimed the quarter hour. She mustn't miss the post.

Sighing softly, she got up, a tall, almost too slender young woman, with a soft, full mouth and vulnerable grey eyes. Her hair was that shade somewhere between blonde and brown. The summer sun had lightened it in places, giving its smooth, straight length a fashionably highlighted effect.

As it swung forwards to obscure her profile she pushed it back off her face with a surprisingly strong and supple hand. Her wrists looked too fragile to support such strength, but her long hours spent working on her tapestries had strengthened the muscles.

This particular commission on which she was working was for a young couple who had recently moved into a large house just outside Bath. He was predictably something in the City. She was pleasant enough, but slightly pretentious. They had two children, both as yet under five, but both boys were down to attend prestigious boarding-schools.

The tapestry, a modern one, was to be the focal point of a large, rectangular, galleried hallway and was to be hung so that it was the first thing that caught the visitor's eye upon entering the house. Jessica had given a good deal of thought to its subject matter.

Arabella Moore had said vaguely that she was quite happy to leave everything to her; she had apparently seen some of her work in the shop in Bath, and had additionally read the very good report that had appeared in a prestigious glossy magazine, praising Jessica's innovative skills.

'Something amusing and witty,' was the only specification Arabella had made, and Jessica only hoped that her client would be happy with her design. As yet she had not started work on the tapestry itself. The design was still very much at the drawing-board stage, awaiting completion then approval from Arabella.

As always when she was engrossed in a project, Jessica resented anything that took her away from it.

As she went to open her workroom door she heard an indignant yowl from outside and grimaced to herself, wondering what trophy Cluny her cat had brought back for her to admire. Cluny had been a stray, rescued one stormy November night, when she had found him crouched, wet and shivering, in her back garden. Now fully grown, he was sleek and black, and full of his own importance.

She opened the door and looked outside, giving a faint sigh of relief at the lack of any small, furry corpse. Cluny was a hunter, and nothing she could say to him seemed to make any difference, so she had had to learn to live with his uncivilised habit of bringing her back gifts of small, pathetic, lifeless bodies.

Everyone had a right to life, she believed that most passionately and intensely, and always had, but her belief had grown stronger and fiercer ever since she herself had come face to face with the realisation that her own life could end between the taking of one breath and the next, and despite the security of her cottage and the sheltered life-style she now lived, seeing only a few close friends, admitting no one new to her circle until she felt completely secure with them, there was still that haunting fear which had never really left her.

It had been a good summer, but now they were into October, and the blue sky beyond her window held the clear pureness that warned of dropping temperatures. She was wearing jeans and a thick woollen sweater, because, despite the fact that the rest of the cottage was centrally heated, she preferred to keep her workroom free of anything that might damage the valuable antique tapestries she sometimes worked on at home.

The cottage had a sharp, narrow flight of stairs which she preferred to keep polished in the old-fashioned way, a central runner kept in place with stair-rods—both the rods and the runner had been lucky finds at an antique fair. The runner, once cleaned, had proved to have a strength of colour which went well with the cottage's oak stairs and floors.

Only one or two of her prospective clients had ever remarked that surely modern fitted carpets would be both warmer and cleaner, and these clients had always proved to be the difficult ones—the ones to whom her work was something that had newly become fashionable and who really had no true appreciation of its history and art.

Downstairs she had a small, comfortable sitting-room with windows overlooking her tiny front garden and beyond it the main road that ran through the village, and a good-sized kitchen-cum-dining-room-cum-sitting-room which she had furnished mainly with antiques picked up here and there from various sales.

Only the kitchen cupboards were modern, and that was because the lack of space forced her to make the maximum use of every corner. Solid oak and limed, they had been built by a local craftsman and added a pleasing lightness to the low-beamed ceilinged room.

A scrubbed farmhouse table divided the kitchen area of the room from the sitting area. She had retained the open fireplace, and alongside it against

the wall was a comfortable sofa draped with a soft
woollen blanket and covered with tapestry cushions.

The stone floor was warmed by a collection of
rugs, but the thing that struck strangers most forc-
ibly about Jessica's home was the startling amount
of vibrant colour. Those who had only met her
outside her home assumed that, because she chose
to wear camouflage colours of beige, olive and
taupe, her home would echo these subtle but sometimes dull shades. Instead, it was full of vibrant
rich reds, blues, greens and golds put so harmoni-
ously together that the surprised visitor came away
with the sensation of having been exposed to something exceptionally alive and warming.

No one was more aware of dichotomy between
her habitat and her personal mode of dress than
Jessica herself. Once, as a child, she had pleaded
with her mother to be allowed to have a rich ruby
velvet dress. She could see it in her mind's eye now,
feel the delicious warmth of the supple fabric, smell
its rich scent. Her mother had been aghast, con-
trolling her own distaste for the dress by gently
pointing her in the direction of another one in
muted olive Viyella. And she had learned then that
little girls who were going to grow up to run a merchant bank did not dress in rich ruby velvet.

Now out of habit rather than anything else she
still wore those same colours gently dictated by her
mother. Not that clothes interested her anyway—
not in the way that fabrics, colours and textures
did. Clothes were simply the means one used to
protect one's body from heat and cold . . . and, in

her case, to provide her with the protection of anonymity.

No one would look twice at a slender young woman, unremarkable of face and figure, dressed in dull, practical clothes. No one would pick her out as a target...a victim...

Her parents had never understood her decision to come and live and work in Avon. They had pleaded with her to change her mind, but she had remained steadfast, and she had had the report of her doctor to back her up. Peace and tranquillity, relief from pressure, a need to recuperate and gather up her mental strength—that was what he had advised.

That had been five years ago. Now her parents accepted, albeit reluctantly, that she lived a different life from theirs.

Her mother had never given up trying to coax her back to London. Every few months she had a fresh attempt—still hoping, perhaps, for that all-important grandson—but Jessica shied away from the commitment that marriage involved. She was free for the first time in her life, and that was the way she intended to stay. Marriage meant responsibilities, duties, putting others' feelings first... She didn't want that.

In her hall she picked up her parcel and let herself out into the small front garden. The sun was warm, but the air cool once she stepped into the shadows. She paused to admire the dwarf Michaelmas daisies she had planted much earlier in the year. Their rich massing of purple, mauve and lilac pleased her and she bent to touch their petals gently. Gardening was her second love, and she planted her garden in much the same way as she worked on her tapestries, but with the artist's fine eye for colour and form.

The post office was the only shop in the village; the nearest garage was ten miles away in the small market town, and the post office was very much the focus of village life. Mrs Gillingham, who ran it, knew all the local gossip and passed it on to her customers with genial impartiality. Jessica interested her. It was unusual for so young and pretty a woman to live so very much alone. Martha Gillingham put her single state down to a broken romance in her past, romantically assuming that it was this relationship which had led to her arrival in the village and to her single state.

She was quite wrong.

Jessica had never been in love. Initially because there had never been time. At university she had worked desperately hard for her degree, terrified of disappointing her parents' hopes for her, and then when she joined the bank everyone had known exactly who she was—the daughter of the bank's chairman—and that knowledge had isolated her from the other young people working there.

And then, after what had happened, the last thing on her mind had been falling in love. She liked her single state and was content with it, but something in the speculative way Mrs Gillingham always questioned her about her private life made her feel raw and hurt inside, as though the postmistress had uncovered a wound she hadn't known was there.

Not that there was anything malicious in her questions. She was just inquisitive, and over the years Jessica had learned to parry them with tact and diplomacy.

Today she had the attention of the postmistress to herself. She was just waiting for her parcel to be weighed when she felt the cold rush of air behind her as the door opened.

The postmistress stopped what she was doing to smile warmly at the newcomer, exclaiming, 'Good morning, Mr Hayward! Are you all settled in yet?'

'Not yet, I'm afraid.'

The man had a deep, pleasant voice, and even without looking at him Jessica knew that he was smiling. She had heard from the milkman about this newcomer who had moved into the once lovely, but now derelict Carolean house on the outskirts of the village, but so far she hadn't actually met him.

'In fact, I was wondering if you could help me,' he was saying, and then added, 'but please finish serving this young lady first.'

The faint touch of reproof in his voice startled Jessica, giving the words far more than the form of mere good manners.

She turned round instinctively and was confronted by a tall, almost overpoweringly male man, dressed in jeans similar to her own and a thick sweater over a woollen shirt, his dark hair flecked with what looked like spots of white paint, and a rather grim expression in his eyes.

There was something about him that suggested that he wasn't the kind to suffer fools gladly. All Jessica knew about him was that he had bought the house at auction, and that he was planning to vir-

tually camp out in it while the builders worked to
make it habitable.

He had arrived in the village only that weekend,
and had apparently been having most of his meals
at the Bell, the local pub, because the kitchen up
at the house was unusable.

She had heard that he worked in London, and
that being the case Jessica would have thought it
would be more sensible of him to stay there at least
until such time as his house was habitable.

Mrs Gillingham had finished weighing the parcel,
and, summing up the situation with a skilled and
speedy eye, quickly performed introductions, giving
Jessica no option but to take the hard brown hand
extended to her and to respond to his quick 'Please
call me Daniel,' with a similarly friendly gesture.

'Jessica Collingwood . . .' His eyebrows drew together briefly, as though somehow he was disconcerted, the pressure of his grip hardening slightly,
and then he was relaxing, releasing her and saying
evenly, 'Jessica—it suits you.'

And yet Jessica had the impression that the
flattery was an absent-minded means of deflecting
her attention away from that momentary tense surprise that had leapt to his eyes as he'd repeated her
name.

Mrs Gillingham, eyeing them with satisfaction,
went on enlighteningly. 'Jessica makes tapestries,
Mr Hayward. You'll have to go and look at her
work,' she added archly. 'It's just the sort of thing
you're going to need for that house of yours.'

Jessica gritted her teeth at this piece of arch manipulation and hoped that Daniel Hayward would realise that this arrant piece of salesmanship was not at *her* instigation.

It seemed he did, because he gave her a warm, reassuring smile and then said ruefully, 'Unfortunately, before I can hang any tapestries on them I'm going to have to have some walls. This...' he touched his hair gingerly '...is the result of an unsafe ceiling collapsing on me this morning.' His face suddenly went grim and Jessica shivered, recognising that here was the real man, the pure male essence of him in the hard, flat determination she could read in his eyes.

'I've sacked the builder I was using for negligence, and I was hoping you might be able to give me the names of some others from whom I might get estimates...'

Mrs Gillingham pursed her mouth, trying not to look flattered by this appeal. 'Well, there's Ron Todd. He does a lot of work hereabouts...and then there's that man you had to do your kitchen, Jessica. What's his name?'

'Alan Pierce,' Jessica informed her, helplessly being drawn into the conversation, wanting to stay and bask in the warm admiration she could read so clearly in Daniel Hayward's lion-gold eyes, and at the same time wanting desperately to escape before she became helplessly involved in something she sensed instinctively was dangerous.

'Oh, yes, that's it... Well, he's very good. Made a fine job of Jessica's kitchen. You ought to see it...'

Numbly Jessica recognised that she was being given a very firm push in the direction Mrs Gillingham had decided she was going to take.

No need to enquire if Daniel Hayward was married or otherwise attached. Mrs Gillingham was a strict moralist, and if she was playing match-maker then it could only be in the knowledge that he was single.

Helplessly, torn between anger and a strange, sweet stirring of excited pleasure, she found herself stumblingly inviting Daniel to call round and see how Alan Pierce had transformed her two small, dark rooms into her large, comfortable living kitchen.

'But, of course ... you must be busy ... and ...'

He started to say that he wasn't, when suddenly the post office door banged open.

A man came in, masked and holding a gun. He motioned to them all with it and said gutturally, 'Over there, all of you!'

Mrs Gillingham was protesting shrilly. At her side, Jessica was dimly conscious of Daniel Hayward's protective bulk coming between her and the man, but he couldn't protect her! Nothing could. It was her worst nightmare come back to haunt her. She started to tremble, dragged back into that time in the past—that awful, unforgettable day that had changed the whole course of her life ...

CHAPTER TWO

JESSICA had left for work at eight o'clock as she always did. She liked to arrive at the bank at the same time as the other staff. Her father arrived later, his chauffeur dropping him off outside the bank's premises at about nine-thirty.

There was nothing remarkable about the day. It was late March, cold and blustery still, with no real hint of spring. She was wrapped up against the cold wind in the navy wool coat which seemed to be the uniform of ambitious, career-minded young women, her hair styled sleekly in the expensive bob that her parents liked so much, its colour subtly enlivened by monthly visits to an expensive Knightsbridge hairdresser.

Beneath her coat she was wearing a navy businesslike suit and a striped cotton blouse which more resembled a man's shirt than a woman's.

On her feet she had good quality, low-heeled leather pumps, and when she got on the tube she mingled anonymously into the crowd of similarly dressed young women.

The bank, like others of its kind, was situated inside that part of London known as the 'City', several streets off Threadneedle Street, taking up a prominent corner position in a small square.

The commissionaire greeted Jessica with a smile that held just that hint of knowing deference. She was acutely conscious of the fact that, while she was *supposed* to be treated just as any other junior member of the staff, she was in fact being handled cautiously with kid gloves not just by her fellow workers, but also by her superiors, all of whom were very conscious of the fact that she was the chairman's daughter.

It wasn't an enviable position, despite what some of her contemporaries thought—she had overheard one of the other girls making catty remarks about her in the cloakroom. She felt set apart from the other girls, alien to them, all too aware of their muted hostility.

Not that being her father's daughter actually afforded her the type of privileges they seemed to think. In the evening, when they were out discoing and enjoying themselves, *she* was at home being catechised by her father as to what she had learned. Her degree did not exempt her from sitting all her Institute exams, and she was all too conscious that he was expecting her to do well.

The pressure on her, well-meant and proud though it was, kept her weight a little under what it ought to be for her height. Even now, early in her working day, she was conscious of an unhealthy tension across her shoulder-blades.

Tonight was the night she went to advanced evening classes for embroidery; the one bright shining pleasure in her otherwise tension-filled week.

She knew that, no matter how much she strove, working in the bank was never going to be anything other than a duty, and a reluctant one at that, but she just couldn't bring herself to disappoint her parents—especially her father—by telling them that she could not fulfil their ambitions for her.

This particular morning there was no commissionaire on duty, but when she turned the handle on the door of the back entrance to the bank, which the staff used on arriving and leaving, she found that the door was unlocked.

She walked into the familiar Stygian darkness of the narrow Victorian passage that led to the offices and cubby-holes at the back of the banking hall proper.

The first thing that struck her as she emerged into the general office was the silence . . . the second was the group of masked, armed men, one of whom was advancing grimly towards her, the rest holding the other members of the staff in a silent, threatened group.

'Get over there and keep your mouth closed.'

Her body trembling with shock, she did as she was instructed. It took several seconds for it to fully dawn on her that this was that most dreaded of all events within the banking community—an armed bank raid.

In such events, all bank staff were instructed not to try to do anything that might risk either their lives or those of others.

As she joined the silent group, Jessica saw that her father's second in command was among them, his normally highly coloured fleshy features a shade of old tallow. As her father's second in command he was in charge of one set of vault keys, while the bank accountant held the other. Together every morning they would unlock the vault so that the cashiers could collect cash for their tills.

Whenever necessary, and never normally on a regular basis, fresh supplies of cash were delivered from the nearby Bank of England. Only yesterday, late in the afternoon after close of banking hours, they had received an exceptionally large consignment of cash, and Jessica realised in sick fear that somehow the thieves must have known of this.

In retrospect, the ordeal of waiting while each member of staff arrived and was duly imprisoned with his or her colleagues seemed to be dragged out over a lifetime of unimaginable terror and shock.

None of them had any way of knowing what was to happen to them...whether they would all emerge unharmed from their ordeal.

On this particular day, Jessica knew that her father was not due into the bank until after lunch, having a morning appointment with an important customer. It seemed the thieves knew it as well, because just as soon as they were sure that all the staff had arrived they took them all at gunpoint to one of the large safes beneath the branch and shut them in it under armed guard.

Still forbidden to speak, and under the silent, masked threat of the gunmen facing them, they felt tension fill the room like a sour taste in the air.

All of them were close to breaking-point, but still it came as something of a shock when one of the other girls, the one who had been so catty about her working in the bank, suddenly called out frantically to their guard, '*She's* the one you ought to be concentrating on. She's the chairman's daughter. She's far more use to you than we are.'

Jessica held her breath, her chest painfully tight with anxiety and fear as the gunman turned slowly in her direction. Through the slits in his mask, she could see the icy glitter of his eyes. He motioned to her to step forward. When she hesitated, John Knowles, the accountant, bravely stepped in front of her, saying quickly, 'She's just a girl. Let her be.'

When the gunman hit him on the side of his head with the butt of his gun, a massed audible breath of shock rippled through them all.

Shaking with tension, Jessica obeyed the gunman's instruction to step forward. He walked slowly round her, the sensation of him standing behind her making the hairs rise in the nape of her neck.

So this was terror, this thick, cold sensation that bordered on paralysis, freezing the body and yet leaving the mind sharply clear to assimilate the vulnerabilities of her position.

The sound of the safe door opening took the gunman from behind her to join his fellow members of the gang. In the low-toned conversation they exchanged Jessica caught her own name, but not much else, and then to her horror she was being told to walk towards them. Flanked on either side by a gunman, she was escorted from the safe.

Hearing the safe door clang closed behind her was the very worst sound she had ever heard. Behind that closed door were her colleagues, safe now, surely, while she . . .

'Better take her upstairs to the boss,' the second gunman instructed the first.

The 'boss' was a powerfully built man with the coldest, shrewdest eyes she had ever seen.

'Chairman's daughter, is she?' he repeated when informed of her status.

'Yeah. I thought we could get a good ransom.'

A quick turn of the 'boss's' hand silenced her jailer.

'We'll take her with us,' the 'boss' announced chillingly after studying her for several seconds. 'She can be our insurance.'

What followed still haunted her in her nightmares. Blindfolded and gagged, she was bundled out of the bank and directly into the kind of armoured vehicle normally used by security companies. Once inside she could sense the presence of other people, even though they remained silent.

The van was driven away and she heard someone saying, 'How long do you reckon before anyone can raise the alarm?'

'Bank's supposed to be open in five minutes. That should give us half an hour or so before anyone realises what's happened... It will take them a fair time to break into the safe. The only other set of keys are held by the chairman, and he's out in Kent.'

'By the time they do get hold of them we'll——'

A sudden curse obviously reminded the speaker of her presence and he fell silent. She was sitting on the floor of the van, bound, blindfolded and gagged. Her body ached from the pressure of the hard floor and the fear-induced tension. She was sure she was going to die, to become another statistic of violence and greed, and when the van finally stopped and she was bundled out and half dragged, half carried up flight after flight of stairs and then pushed in a dank, foul-smelling room she was even more convinced that this was the end.

She heard the door close but dared not move, not knowing how many members of the gang were preserving a silent vigil around her. The silence went on and on, a relentless pressure against her stretched eardrums, like a soundless, high-pitched scream, battering at her senses.

Time lost all meaning. Her arms and hands were numb, but still she dared not move, picturing the armed man perhaps sitting in front of her, watching her. Her throat was dry and sore, but she couldn't ask for a drink. Her body ached, and cramp ran like a violent wrenching wire from her left calf to her ankle.

Outwardly motionless and controlled, inwardly she was falling apart, suffering the most appalling imagined fates, wondering if whoever had said those immortal words 'a brave man dies once, the coward a thousand times over' had really any awareness of the true terrors created by the imagination—terrors which had nothing whatsoever to do with one's ability to endure actual physical pain.

At some point she slipped into a semi-comatose state that gave her some relief, a sort of self-induced, drugged miasma of mental agony which separated her from her physical body and its discomforts. She couldn't move at all... couldn't do anything other than sit there where she had been left, straining her ears for some other movement in the room.

Quite when she began to realise she might be on her own she had no idea; perhaps it was when the quality of the silence struck her as being empty. She held her breath, listening anxiously for the sound of other breath, trying not to imagine the grinning faces of the gang while they witnessed her pathetic attempts to use what senses were left to her to work out if they were there.

If they were there... She was almost sure they weren't. Which meant... which meant that she was alone.

She ought to have felt relief, but instead she felt all the blind, frantic panic of a helpless child deserted by its parents. She couldn't move—her wrists were bound and so were her ankles, and her wrists were tied to some kind of pipe.

She heard a noise—not a human sound... The hairs on her arms stood up in terror as she felt something run across her bare leg. She wanted desperately to scream, but couldn't remove the gag nor scream through it.

Panic engulfed her; she tried desperately to pull herself free, and succeeded only in rubbing her wrists raw on their bonds so that the broken skin bled.

After panic and terror came dull, destructive acceptance. She was going to die here in this unknown place, and she might as well resign herself to it.

How long had she been here already? Hours... but how many?

She tried to think constructively, but it was impossible. All she wanted now was oblivion, escape...

When the door finally opened, her rescuers were all moved to different degrees of shock and pity by what they saw.

A telephone call to the bank had announced that any attempt to find her or them during the next five hours would result in her death, but that if no attempt was made to track them down for that period then her father would be informed of where she could be found.

Since the police had no idea of where to start looking for the thieves, they had had no option other than to comply with their demands, and against all their expectations they had actually received the promised call later in the day giving the address of a slum-clearance flat in a high-rise block where she could be found.

To Jessica, the debriefing that followed her imprisonment was almost as gruelling as the imprisonment itself, although in a different way.

The whole nightmare affair had left her perilously close to the edge of a complete mental and physical breakdown, with the result that she had finally told her parents that she could not return to the bank, and that instead she was going to use the small inheritance left to her by her maternal grandparents to train for a career much more suited to her now fierce determination to live as quiet and safe a life as possible.

Of course her parents had protested, especially when they had learned she intended moving to Avon.

There was no reason why she couldn't continue to live at home in London and practise her career from there, they told her, but she refused to be swayed. London was now a place that terrified her. She couldn't walk down a busy street without being overcome by the feeling that someone was walking behind her, stalking her—without the fear she had known in that small, frightening prison coming back to drag her back down into the pit of self-destructive fear she was only just beginning to leave behind.

In the end her parents had reluctantly given way on the advice of her doctor, who had told them that she needed to find a way of healing herself and coming to terms with what had happened.

That healing process was still going on, and now, suddenly and shockingly, she had been dragged back into that remembered horror.

She saw the gunman coming towards her and started to scream. He lashed out at her with the butt of his gun. She felt a stunning pain like fire in her shoulder, followed by a cold wash of paralysing weakness, and knew that she was going to faint.

When she came round, the small post office was full of people. She was lying on the floor with something under her head and someone kneeling beside her holding her wrist while he measured her pulse.

She looked up cold with fear, trembling with the remembered shock of the past, and encountered the warm gold eyes of Daniel Hayward. His look of warmth and compassion was reassuring and comforting. She tried to sit up, conscious of her undignified prone position and the curious glances of the people standing around her.

As she looked round the shop, Daniel Hayward seemed to know what she was looking for and said quietly, 'It's all right. He's gone.'

'Gone?'

She looked bewildered, and it was left to Mrs Gillingham to explain excitedly, 'Mr Hayward was ever so brave. He reached right out and took the gun off him, and told me to open the door and shout for help.'

While Jessica looked uncomprehendingly at him, he said humorously, 'Not brave, really. I simply made use of the excellent distraction you provided by drawing our friend's fire, although such a course of action is not really to be recommended. You'll be lucky if your arm isn't out of action for a good few days, I'm afraid.'

Her arm... Jessica tried to lift it and gasped as the pain coursed like fire though the bruised muscles.

'It's all right...nothing's actually broken,' Daniel Hayward was telling her reassuringly. 'But that was a nasty blow you took, and there's bound to be some very considerable bruising. Look,' he offered quietly, 'why don't you let me take you home? I've got my car outside. Mrs Gillingham has sent someone to fetch the doctor, but I think you'll feel

much more comfortable lying on your own bed than
lying here . . .'

He was so understanding, so concerned, so gentle
in the way that he touched her, gently helping her
to her feet. She couldn't ever remember a man
treating her like this before, nor herself wanting one
to. Almost instinctively she leaned against him,
letting him take her slender weight as he guided her
towards the door, politely refusing the offers of help
showered on them both.

'I suspect the police will probably want to interview you later,' he told her gently as he settled her
in the passenger seat of an immaculate and brand
new Daimler saloon. Her father always drove a
Daimler, and she was aware of a certain, unexpected nostalgic yearning for her parents' presence
as he set the car in motion.

The last time she had seen them had been
Christmas, when she had paid a reluctant duty visit
to her old home. She had been on edge and nervous
the whole time she was there—not so much because
of her old fear of London's crowds and anonymity,
she had recognised in some surprise, but because
of her deep-rooted guilt, and fear that somehow or
other her parents would succeed in gently pres-
suring her into returning to her old life . . . a life she
knew she could no longer tolerate because of the
restrictions it placed upon her.

Although the gulf between them saddened her,
although she was still consumed with guilt in
knowing that she had let them down, she still found
her new life immensely fulfilling—immensely sat-
isfying and pleasing in an entirely personal and dif-

ficult-to-explain way, other than to say it was as though she had now found a piece of herself which had previously been missing, and that in doing so she had completed her personality, making it whole.

'Which house is it?' Daniel Hayward asked her. 'Mrs G said it was along here somewhere...'

She gathered her thoughts and indicated which house was hers, conscious of the discreet twitching of curtains as he stopped the Daimler outside and then got out.

Her neighbours were elderly and very kind, and would doubtless be all agog with curiosity and shock once they heard what had happened.

It had been idiotic of her to react like that. The man had obviously not been much of a threat after all, but she had panicked remembering...

'I think I'd better carry you inside,' Daniel told her easily. 'You still look pretty groggy.'

She wanted to protest, but she felt too weak, her body fluid and amorphous as he swung her up into his arms. It was only a short distance to her front door, but long enough for her to feel the measured beat of his heart and to register the strength in the arms which held her.

Such intimacy with another human being was alien and unfamiliar to her, and yet beneath the rapid thudding of her pulse, beneath the dregs of fear induced by the attempted robbery, and beneath even the instinctive, defensive coiling of her muscles as they locked in protest against the sensation of being so completely within the physical power of someone else, ran another feeling, slow, golden, like a full and lazy river warmed by a summer's heat, its flow so deceptively slow that one wasn't aware of the relentlessness of its strength until it was too late to swim against it.

Her heart seemed to miss a beat and then another; her fingers curled into the roughness of his sweater, and, as though he sensed what was running through her mind and the enormity of her struggle to comprehend the bewildering range of the conflicting emotions she was suffering, he looked at her, the golden eyes calm and gentle, almost as though he knew her fear and was reassuring her.

As he unlocked the door to her house and carried her inside she had the crazy feeling that an intimacy had been born between them that cut through the normal barriers of convention and defensiveness which held the sexes apart. It was as though at some very deep level they had reached out and communicated wordlessly with one another, and that that communication held a silent promise for both their futures. What futures? She was alone, independent, by preference, by choice.

It was odd to hear him ask her quite mundanely, 'Shall I help you upstairs, or...?'

She shook her head.

'No... The sofa in the kitchen will be just as comfortable as my bed,' she told him quickly. 'It's through that door.'

He put her down and then announced that he intended to stay with her until the doctor arrived to check her over, softening his statement with a warm smile. In repose his face possessed a hard purposefulness which in other circumstances would

have repelled her. It made him look too much like
the fiercely competitive and power-hungry men who
moved in her parents' social circle.

The thought disconcerted her, and as he released
her he frowned and asked curtly, 'What's wrong?
Did I hurt you?'

The words seemed to echo warningly inside her,
making her shiver with the knowledge of how easily
this man *could* hurt her, and then she looked up at
him and saw only the concern softening the
harshness of his face, and the anxiety shadowing
the clear golden warmth of his eyes.

She shook her head, half marvelling at how at
ease she felt with him, almost as though he were
an old and valued friend.

But he was a stranger—outwardly at least—and
she was perhaps reading more into his kindness than
she ought, taking up more of his time than she
ought, allowing him far more into her life than she
ought.

As she struggled to thank him and offer him an
opportunity to leave, he stunned her by taking hold
of her hands and holding them firmly within the
grip of his own.

'I'm staying,' he told her evenly.

His palms were slightly calloused, the strength in
his grip reminding her of his maleness. Comforting
her. In reality the last thing she wanted was to be
left alone to relive the horror of that other time...to
remember the choking, destructive horror of the
fear she had experienced then. That must be why
she felt almost like clinging to him, why she wanted
to be with him.

While they were waiting for the doctor he made them both a cup of tea, nodding approvingly when he saw the squat canisters with their differing blends of leaves so much more flavorsome than the dull uniformity of mass-produced tea-bags.

The one he chose, Russian Caravan, was one of her own favourites, drunk piping hot, its taste sharpened with a slice of lemon.

He let her sip hers in silence and then said, complimenting her, 'I like this room. It's comfortable...lived in. It has the kind of ambiance I want for my own place.'

Jessica laughed, amused that this obviously wealthy man whose house, even in its present state of dereliction, was far grander than her own small cottage should admire her simple décor.

'I should have thought for a house like yours you'd have wanted to get in interior designers,' she commented.

To her surprise he shook his head.

'No. The house is going to be my home, not a set piece that looks like a photograph out of a glossy magazine. Mind you, I'm a long way from the decorating and furnishing stage as yet. As I discovered this morning, there's some pretty bad damp damage, and an awful lot of restoration work to be done, simply to bring the fabric of the building up to scratch. At the moment I'm virtually camped out in a couple of rooms.' He grimaced wryly. 'I was hoping to get the worst of the repairs over before Christmas, that's why I'm so damned annoyed with this builder.'

'Wouldn't it have been more sensible to stay in London at least until the house is habitable?' Jessica asked him, curiosity about him overcoming the dull ache in her arm.

'Sensible, perhaps,' he agreed. 'But there comes a time when living and working at the hectic pace demanded by city life begins to pall. My business necessitates my working in the City, but I don't have to live there. Once I'd made the choice to move out...' He shrugged meaningfully, and Jessica guessed that he was a man who, once he had made a decision, seldom changed his mind.

'Your business...?' she asked and then hesitated, wondering if her questions were too intrusive. She had never felt anything to match the fierce need she was now experiencing to know everything there was to know about this man. He filled her senses, absorbing her attention to the exclusion of everything else, and these sensations were a phenomenon to her. She found it hard to understand how she, normally so cautious in her dealings with others, could feel so at ease with this stranger, and yet at the same time so keyed up, so buoyed up by his presence that everything in her life now seemed to be coloured by her reactions to him.

She sensed his hesitation in answering her question and flushed uncomfortably. Was she being too pushy, too inquisitive? After all, she had no previous experience to go on—no past relationships in her life to show her how to deal with the sensations he was arousing inside her.

But at last he answered her, his voice oddly sombre as he told her almost reluctantly, 'I'm an economist. I work in the City.'

An economist. She guessed vaguely that he was probably involved in some way with the stock market, and, knowing how secretive people involved in the sales of stocks and shares sometimes had to be, she felt she could understand his reticence and quickly changed the subject.

'Quite a few City people have moved out this way recently, although we are a bit off the beaten track. It isn't unknown for the village to be snowed in in a bad winter,' she warned him, but he laughed and seemed unconcerned by the threat of not being able to reach the City.

'What about you?' he challenged her. 'I've already heard all about your tapestries. In fact, I suspect that the marvellous creation I recently admired hanging on a friend's wall was designed and made by you, but surely from a selling point of view you'd do better living somewhere, if not central to London, then, say, like Bath, where there's a thriving interior decoration industry.'

'I don't like cities...or crowds,' she told him shortly. The ache in her shoulder was nagging painfully. 'I prefer to live somewhere quiet.'

'And isolated?' he probed skilfully, the golden eyes watching her as she looked at him in startled defensiveness. 'It wasn't so difficult to deduce,' he told her gently, as though answering her unspoken question. 'A very attractive and clever young woman living alone in a tiny rural village; a young woman whom it is obvious was not born and bred here, and whose skills have a much wider field of demand than her environs suggest. What happened?' he asked gently.

Tears clogged her throat. This was the first time anyone had asked her about the past; the first time anyone had seen past her defences and guessed that there was more to her desire to live so quietly than merely a love of the Avon countryside. She wanted to tell him, and yet conversely was afraid to do so. Why? In case he dismissed her fears as trivial and foolish as her parents had done? In case he was embarrassed by them as her London friends had been? Or just in case he simply did not understand the trauma of what she had endured and how it had affected her?

Panic suddenly overwhelmed her, followed by the old dread of talking to anyone about what she had endured—a fear which her doctor told her probably sprang from an atavistic belief that, in somehow refusing to talk about her ordeal, she was succeeding in shutting herself off from it, and that her reluctance to talk about it sprang from a deep-rooted dread that, once she did, her old terror would mushroom and overwhelm her, growing beyond her control to the point where it dragged her down and consumed her.

Her throat muscles locked, her body suddenly tense as she sat crouched on the sofa, defensive and inarticulate, the half of her brain that could still reason knowing that he must be wondering what on earth he had said to spark off such a reaction, and dreading him withdrawing from her.

A sound beyond the room distracted him. He lifted his head, frowning, and then said quietly, 'I think the doctor has probably arrived. I'll go and let him in.'

Tactfully he offered to leave her alone with the doctor, but she shook her head, wanting his presence, feeling protected and comforted by it, and yet at the same time feeling guilty, because she was imposing on him.

When she tried to say as much he shook his head and then took hold of both her hands, saying quietly, 'No, never... I want to stay.'

And then he smiled at her, and in the warmth of his eyes she saw a promise that dazzled and awed her. He shared her awareness of that instant and shocking recognition, that sensation of feeling inexplicably attuned to one another. She had heard of people falling in love at first sight. Was this what had happened to them?

But falling in love was an ephemeral, laughable thing that only happened to the reckless and impulsive, and she was neither of those. There was nothing shallow about the way she felt about him. No. This was more than a sense of recognition, of knowing that here was a man who seemed to understand, as though by instinct, everything there was to know about her—about her fears and apprehensions, about her weaknesses and strengths. Indeed, it was almost as though he possessed some deep inner knowledge of her that enabled him to recognise her every emotion and feeling.

He deliberately busied himself clearing away their china mugs and emptying the teapot while the doctor asked her to remove her sweater and examined her injured shoulder and arm.

Already both were painfully swollen, showing evidence of the bruising that was yet to come.

'Mm... Nothing's broken, but you're going to find that arm painful and stiff for a few days, I'm afraid. I think it might be as well to rest it in a sling at least for the next forty-eight hours.'

It would have to be her right arm, Jessica reflected wryly as the doctor rummaged in his bag for an antiseptic pack containing the requisite sling.

'I can leave you some pain-killers,' he suggested, eyeing her thoughtfully. 'Generally speaking, when a patient suffers extreme shock as you have done I can prescribe a mild sleeping tablet...'

Jessica shuddered and shook her head. She remembered the drugs she had been prescribed before, supposedly to help her sleep, but which in reality had doped and numbed her to such an extent that they had actually intensified her struggle to come to terms with her residual fear once she was without the crutch they offered.

'Sensible girl,' the doctor approved. 'A mild sedative isn't necessarily addictive, but I don't like prescribing them unless it's absolutely essential. If you want my advice, perhaps a good tot of brandy in your bedtime cocoa is just as effective.'

And equally addictive, Jessica thought to herself, but he was an old-fashioned doctor, with his patients' welfare very much at heart.

He closed his bag and turned to leave, pausing by the door to frown and ask, 'You live here alone, don't you?'

Jessica nodded, a cold finger of ice touching her spine, and she asked quickly, 'What's wrong? The man didn't escape, did he? I thought...'

'No, nothing like that,' he was quick to reassure her. 'It's just that with that arm you might be better having someone staying here overnight with you. Just in case you're tempted to dispense with the sling and overstrain the muscle. I could have a word with Mrs G——'

'There's no need,' Daniel intervened unexpectedly. 'I shall be staying here tonight.'

Jessica gasped, but the small sound was lost as the doctor nodded his approval and opened the door saying, 'No... No, there's no need to see me out. Nasty business altogether. Who'd have thought, in a small village like this...? Lucky thing you acted so promptly, young man...'

His voice faded away as Daniel ignored his protests and escorted him to the door. Jessica waited tensely as the door closed and she heard Daniel walking back to the kitchen.

'Yes. I know,' he said calmly as he came in. 'I jumped in there without consulting you, but I thought you'd prefer my presence to that of Mrs G, good neighbour though she is. If I was wrong...'

Jessica shook her head. He wasn't wrong at all, but they hardly knew one another. Until a few short hours ago they had been strangers, and, despite the fact that she felt drawn to him in a way she had never before experienced, the habits of a lifetime could not be so easily overthrown. She plucked nervously at her sweater with fingers that trembled a little, unable to bring herself to look at him in case she saw mockery in those too perceptive gold eyes.

'You're worried about what people might say about my staying here, is that it?' he asked her quietly.

Instantly her head shot up, her eyes blazing with pride and anger.

'Certainly not,' she told him curtly. 'I'm not so narrow-minded nor insular. I prefer to set my own standards for the way I live my life, not pay lip-service to other people's.'

'Then what *are* you afraid of?' he asked her gently, dropping down on to the sofa beside her, sitting so close to her that she could feel the heat passing from his body to her own, an unnerving, vibrant male heat that made her body quicken and her muscles tense—in expectation, not fear. 'Not me, surely?'

How could she tell him it was herself she feared, and her out-of-character reactions to him?

'I'm just not used to sharing my home with anyone,' she told him evasively.

'I'm invading your privacy, and you're not sure how you feel about it, is that it? Well, I can understand that. Like you I, too, prize my solitude. Like you I've always preferred to live alone. However, there comes a time . . .'

His voice had slowed and deepened. Without looking at him she sensed that he had moved closer to her, felt it in the warm vibration of his breath against her temple, and quivered in silent reaction to it.

When he reached for her hand she let him take it, even though she knew what her trembling would reveal to him.

With his other hand he cupped her face and turned it so that he could look at her. The warm grasp of his hand was somehow reassuring, as though he knew what she was feeling.

'If I'm presuming too much . . . if I'm letting my own feelings and reactions blind me into believing that what's happening between us is mutual, then tell me so, Jessica.'

An idiotic shyness swamped her, and it was as much as she could do to shake her head, her throat clogged with emotional tension.

'There are so many things we still have to learn about one another . . . so many things we still don't know or share, but there will be time for us to discover and learn all those things. For now shall we simply let it be enough that we're here together at the beginning of a journey we both want to share?'

Gratefully Jessica nodded her head.

He was telling her that he wasn't going to rush or pressure her. He seemed to know how unused she was to everything that was happening to her, how alarmed she was by it, at the same time as she thrilled to the knowledge that he shared her feeling; she who had never wanted this kind of involvement suddenly wanted it desperately.

As she looked at him, she wondered blindingly what it would be like when he kissed her, and as though he had read the question in her eyes his own suddenly darkened awesomely.

'Don't,' he warned her huskily, and then added, 'Once I start touching you I shan't be able to stop.'

Shockingly, her body responded to his warning so intensely that for a moment she was almost tempted into reckless incitement of the desire she saw burning in his eyes. She looked at his mouth and felt her body tremble. She reached out to touch her fingers to the male texture of his lips, to explore their shape and form, and then sanity prevailed and she drew back, her face betraying her own bewilderment.

Fighting to master the temptation flooding her, she said unsteadily, 'Tell me about your house. How did you find it? What do you plan to do with it? You're our first really local migrant from London, you realise. There are others, but they live on the other side of Blanchester. What brought you out as far as this?'

She was desperately trying to distract herself, to bring herself back on an even keel, and so missed the sudden tension of his body, the brief hesitation as he replied, 'Chance, really. I'd been looking for a house outside London for some time, and then someone mentioned this village.'

'Someone mentioned it?' Jessica looked at him, frowning, and then her frown cleared. 'Oh, you mean your estate agents. Well, they must have been relieved to have sold the Court. It's been empty for almost two years, and it's been badly vandalised.'

'You don't have to tell me that,' Daniel told her wryly. 'When you feel up to it, I'd like to have your views on how best to redesign the kitchen. My existing builder is a bit short on imagination, and

I want to avoid the stereotyped blandness so preva-
lent among kitchen designers. It will be a good-
sized room: two rooms, really, since I'm having the
wall between it and what was at one time, the
housekeeper's room knocked down.'

Gradually the sexual tension was easing from her
body, to be replaced by a genuine interest in his
plans for the house. When he glanced at his watch
and informed her that it was almost seven o'clock
she could hardly believe it.

'Will you be OK if I leave you for long enough
to go and collect a few things?' he asked her. 'I
could ask Mrs G to sit with you...'

Jessica shook her head. 'I'll be fine. Really, you
don't need to stay overnight. I——'

'I'm staying,' he told her gently. 'And don't you
dare move from that sofa until I get back. Remember what the doctor said about not straining
the muscles.'

It wasn't very difficult to obey him; in fact, it
wasn't any hardship at all to simply sit there and
give in to the luxury of day-dreaming about the
promises that had been implicit in almost everything he had said to her.

She had never believed this would happen to
her—that she would meet someone and fall in love
so quickly and intensely that within a few short
hours it would be impossible to imagine her life
without him—but it *had* happened, and not just to
her, but to him as well.

She closed her eyes and gave in to the temptation
of imagining what it would feel like to have his
mouth moving on hers, his hands touching her skin,

exploring her body with all the delicate skill his touch had already promised.

A rash of goose-bumps broke out under her skin, a tense, coiling sensation invading her lower stomach.

Physical desire... Up until now she had been a stranger to such feelings, so what was it about this particular man encountered in such harrowing circumstances that had led to its birth now?

Were the feelings, both emotional and physical, which she was experiencing genuine, or were they some kind of by-product of her fear?

Deep within her a part of herself recognised that alongside her burgeoning happiness ran a fine thread of cautious reluctance, as though that part of her was unwilling to allow itself to be committed to what she was feeling for Daniel.

She was too exhausted to dwell on the matter. Upstairs in her workroom, the phone rang. That was her business line, and by rights she ought to go up there and answer it. She was doing quite well now, but not so well that she could afford to turn down business.

Daniel had been so kind to her. So caring. Surely far more so than she, as a stranger to him, merited, and it struck her that he himself must be a very well-adjusted human being to be able to reach out so readily and warmly to a stranger, disregarding the possibility of their rejection. She realised that in similar circumstances she would most probably not have offered the same Good-Samaritan-inspired kindness, not because she would not have wanted to, but because she would have been afraid, as she

suspected many people were afraid, of having her
offer misconstrued or, even worse, resented. If she
had spurned Daniel's kindness and retreated into
the prickly sharp shell she normally used to conceal
her true self from strangers, she suspected that he
would have treated her reaction with equally con-
siderate and thoughtful kindness.

He was plainly a man of intense generosity of
spirit, and it humbled her that he should choose to
treat her as his equal when she knew that inwardly
she was nothing of the sort. She tended to hold
even people who knew her at a distance, deliberately refusing to let them trespass too far.

Daniel was the first person in a long time whom
she had actually wanted to draw into her life.

After her ordeal her doctor had explained these
negative feelings as resulting from the long years
of self-induced pressure when she had forced herself
to conform and to be the daughter her parents
wanted her to be. That they were her own form of
rebellion against that stifling pressure.

Now, in retrospect, she felt ashamed of the way
she had panicked this morning. No one else had.
Mrs G, older than her and a lot frailer, had
managed to cope with the situation. Exhaustion was
numbing her brain. She was too tired to think any
longer. She looked at her watch. Daniel had been
gone just over an hour. Where was he? Had he
changed his mind, had second thoughts?

About what? she scoffed to herself. All he had
offered to do was to stay the night with her on a
purely altruistic and non-sexual basis. It was not as

though, after all, he was about to move in with her as her lover.

But if he was—— Abruptly she stifled the thought. It was too soon, much too soon for those kinds of thoughts.

CHAPTER THREE

WHEN Daniel returned Jessica was asleep. He woke her gently, smiling down into her unmasked eyes as they opened and widened in pleased recognition.

'Sorry it took so long, but I had to go to the pub to explain why I wouldn't be in for my usual evening meal. Of course, they'd heard all about the raid and wanted to know if you were all right. Mrs Markham insisted on giving me a couple of cold chicken salads for tonight, and she said to tell you if there's anything at all she can do, any shopping you want done...'

Stupidly, the thought of such kindness made her eyes fill with tears. She only knew the landlady of the local pub very casually, although she had heard that she was a highly organised and very capable woman under whose management the Bell had risen from a rather lacklustre village pub to a favourite eating place for locals in the know.

'Hey, come on... What did I say?' Daniel teased her gently, producing a clean handkerchief and mopping up her tears as easily and casually as though he had been doing it for years; as though he had known for years of this idiotic weakness of hers for bursting into tears every time she saw a sad film or heard or read something that choked her with emotion.

'I forgot to ask earlier,' he added, 'but is there anyone you want to get in touch with?'

'Get in touch with?' She stared at him.

'Yes, you know... your family.'

'My family?' Her frown deepened, and then she said shortly, 'No... No...' Habit prevented her from lying, and forced her to say unevenly, 'My parents...' the words 'wouldn't be interested' stuck in her throat because she knew they weren't true. Her mother would be down here just as fast as her father's chauffeur could bring her, but her mother fussing around her, rallying her, coaxing and persuading her to return to London was the last thing she wanted right now, and besides... besides...

Selfishly, all she wanted was to be with Daniel.

To ease her conscience she told him quickly, 'My parents lead very busy lives. There's no point in worrying them about this. After all, it's only a bit of bruising.'

The look Daniel was giving her made her flush and feel oddly defensive. She had seen his hawk's eyes warm with compassion and concern; she had seen them dark with the beginnings of passion, but now for the first time she was seeing them harden fractionally, as though accusing her. But of what...?

'As you're being kind enough to go to the trouble of staying here tonight to keep an eye on me, the least thing I can do is to provide you with a meal,' she announced brightly, deliberately changing the subject and trying to get up.

'Not tonight, I think,' Daniel admonished her. 'The doctor said you were to rest...remember?'

'He said I was to rest my arm,' Jessica protested, smiling. 'The rest of me is fully functional.'

He had been watching her as she spoke, and suddenly something vibrant and masculine flared in his eyes and his glance dropped quite deliberately to her body, making a caressing and lingering study of its curves and angles before he said softly, 'It's far more than merely functional.' And then, while she was still flushing, he got up and asked, 'Which room am I to sleep in? I'll take this stuff up there out of the way, and then I suggest that for tonight at least we make do with Mrs Markham's excellent chicken and even better apple pie.'

The heat was still coursing through her body in the aftermath of his deliberate erotic scrutiny of her, and it took her several seconds to pull herself together enough to say distractedly, 'Which room? Oh, there are only two. The spare room faces the street.'

Her eyes focused betrayingly on him as he bent to remove his leather holdall from the floor.

The leather was soft and worn, the holdall unadorned with gimmicky logos, unostentatious and battered, but Jessica recognised its quality none the less. She suspected that had she looked inside it she would have seen tucked discreetly almost out of sight a name familiar to her from her father's luggage. It was his proud boast that he had been given his cases second-hand by an uncle, when he first went up to Oxford, and that he still found them far superior to anything that modern science could produce.

Seeing the familiar brown leather reminded her sharply of her parents and of the gulf that lay between them; a gulf she felt it necessary to maintain to preserve her own independence.

Oh, there was no open rift. Whenever her mother could coax her home they welcomed her with open arms, and she knew quite well that nothing would delight her parents more than to have her living with them once more. Nothing . . . unless it was the news that she was married and pregnant with a grandson. A grandson who would take the place in the bank which she had rejected.

The last time she had been home her cousin had been visiting with her parents. Jessica wasn't particularly fond of Emma. Her cousin was the only child of her mother's sister and her husband.

Emma's father was a country solicitor, and comfortably rather than well off. Jessica suspected that Emma had always resented the fact that her aunt and uncle were far more wealthy than her parents.

They had both attended the same private school. There were only a few months' difference in their ages, and while they were at school Emma had often behaved towards her in a way that was spiteful and jealous.

Now they rarely saw one another. Emma worked in a very expensive and up-market Kensington boutique, and she had long ago announced that it was her sole ambition to find a man rich enough to support her in the same style that Jessica's father supported his family.

'But so many marriages end in divorce, and if you don't love him in the first place...' Jessica had objected sharply, shocked by Emma's revelations.

'Judgemental Jessica, all pi and prudery,' Emma had taunted her. 'So what if it does? You can be sure that I'll make sure I don't come out of any divorce without a substantial sum of money. It's all right for you to look down and sneer. You don't know what real life's all about. Your father's a millionaire.'

'Money isn't everything,' Jessica had told her.

Emma had laughed shrilly. 'Only *you* could come out with a statement like that. Of course it isn't to you...'

That had been when they were both eighteen.

Later, after Jessica's ordeal, Emma had come to see her at home. On the verge of getting engaged to an extremely wealthy minor baronet, she had been seething with resentment and anger because her quarry had been snatched out of her grasp at the last moment by his domineering and extremely protective mother. When she heard that Jessica didn't intend returning to the bank, she had been derisive.

'My God...if only I had your opportunities. You're a fool, Jess. Turning your back on the bank and setting yourself up as some dreary little sewing woman. You're a fool. Do you know that?'

Jessica had ignored her jibes about her embroidery skills and refused to rise to her bait, but since then the disaffection between them had grown.

Emma had married, divorced, and was now looking for husband number two, or so Jessica suspected.

'Come back.'

The soft words made her realise that she had drifted off into her own thoughts.

Daniel smiled at her as he picked up his bag. Even beneath his thick sweater, she could discern the powerful play of his muscles.

A weakening sensation invaded her body as she stared at his supple back, imagining how it would look, how it would feel, to have that powerful, lean body close to her own. His skin would feel smooth and warm, like silk—no, not like silk, like the most expensive kind of satin. And beneath it she would be able to feel the hard, padded muscles and the long, male bones.

Her imagination conjured up pictures that made her face go hot. Guiltily she averted her eyes from his body, sternly lecturing herself on her wanton thoughts.

More for distraction than anything else, while he was upstairs she got up and walked over to the sink. She wasn't an invalid, after all. She had simply bruised the muscles in her arm.

She could fill the kettle left-handedly, and set about the preparations for their evening meal.

Cluny came in through the cat flap, miaowing demandingly. Obligingly she went to get a tin of cat food, automatically reaching for it with her right hand, and then stifling a sharp gasp as her bruised muscles locked and went into a stabbing flash of pain. She dropped the tin of cat food, instinctively nursing her bruised shoulder.

When Daniel came quickly into the kitchen, alerted by her cry of distress, he found her kneeling on the floor trying to recover the tin, which had rolled under the table.

'Leave it!' he told her, his voice so sharp and steely that she obeyed it instinctively, her face flushing with mortification as she realised that his tone was more suitable for addressing a recalcitrant insubordinate than a woman who considered herself both mature and under no one's authority other than her own, but before she could voice any protest he was at her side, tugging her to her feet with such concern that she forgot her anger.

'Why on earth didn't you wait?' he chided her when she explained what had happened.

'It's my arm that's bruised, not my legs. And, besides, Cluny was hungry.'

'Cluny?' He looked down and saw the cat, who was fixing him with a basilisk-like stare.

A smile tugged at the corners of his mouth.

'Ah, yes. I see... Cluny... For the tapestries, of course.'

'Yes,' Jessica agreed, pleased that he had recognised the connection. Not many people who were not knowledgeable in her field realised that she had named her cat after the famous Cluny tapestries. She liked the idea that, economist though he was, Daniel had an obviously wide-ranging grasp of things outside his own field. It pointed to a mind quick and generous enough to acknowledge that monetary matters were not necessarily the focus of everyone's life.

'Well, I think that for tonight at least Cluny will have to rely on me for his food.'

'But it seems all wrong, you waiting on me,' she protested as he firmly led her back to the sofa.

'Chauvinist,' he teased, and then added, 'I promise you I'm quite at home in the kitchen. My mother brought us all up to be self-sufficient.'

'All?' Jessica queried curiously.

'Yes. I have two brothers and a sister.'

Her envy showed in her face. 'How lucky you were. I'm an only child.'

'Only child, lonely child?' he hazarded as he opened the can and spooned out the contents into Cluny's bowl.

'Yes, I was. Oh, my mother did her best. She was forever dragging me off to parties, introducing me to the children of friends, but...'

'But?' Daniel queried, looking thoughtfully at her. 'But what? You didn't like them, you pre-ferred your own company, or you wanted to punish your parents for not providing you with brothers and sisters?'

Jessica raised startled eyes to meet his. How had he known that? She had only recently discovered herself what had lain behind her stubborn refusal to break out of her loneliness, and then only by accident.

A chance remark by a client, wryly commenting that her six-year-old was very definitely punishing her for subjecting him to being an only child, had given her a startling and painful insight into her own childhood behaviour.

'It's all right,' Daniel told her kindly, studying her expression. 'I was the eldest in our family and there were times, believe you me, when I came close to hating my parents for providing me with three siblings, especially the twins.'

'Twins?'

'Mmm. David and Jonathon. You can see that my parents have a penchant for biblical names. The twins arrived when I was seven, and Rachel a year later.'

'Do you still resent them?' Jessica asked him curiously. It seemed impossible to imagine the man she had known today resenting anything or anyone.

He laughed. 'Sometimes. When the twins decide to come and dump themselves and their friends on me for unheralded visits as they tended to do when they were at university, but they're both working in the States now. David's a biochemist and Jonathon's in advertising.'

'And your sister . . . Rachel?'

'Ah, Rachel . . . Well, she looks set to surpass the lot of us. She's training to be a surgeon. Following in our father's footsteps, so to speak. He's a GP,' he added by way of explanation.

Jessica frowned. 'Was he disappointed that none of his sons followed him into medicine?'

'Not really. Why should he be?'

It was a question that she wasn't really ready to answer, leading as it must to disclosures about her life which she was not sure she wanted to make.

Daniel was so well adjusted in comparison to herself. How would he view her actions? She trusted his judgement, and yet something held her back from confiding in him, almost as though she were afraid to have her actions weighed and found lacking.

She was deeply conscious of the fact that her ordeal had given her a get-out from the bank which she had been seeking for a long time.

Because of what she had endured, her parents, in their concern for her health, had made it easy for her to follow her own inclinations, and there were occasions like now when she wondered if part of her had not seized on the opportunity which her mental and physical vulnerability had given her, and if she would have had the courage and determination to follow her own path in life without it.

'Something's bothering you,' Daniel said quietly. 'What is it?'

Jessica shook her head and managed a strained smile.

'I always look like this when I'm hungry,' she told him lightly. 'And I've heard that Mrs Markham's apple pie is something very special.'

She could see that he wasn't deceived, and tensed, waiting for him to press her, wondering how she would react, what she would say, but he didn't, and she wasn't sure if it was relief or disappointment she felt when he simply said easily, 'It is. I can vouch for that.'

Half-way through the evening they received a visit from the local police who wanted to take statements from both of them. While Jessica stumbled and hesitated over hers, conscious that she out of the three of them in the post office had been the only one who had panicked, Daniel, in contrast, delivered his calmly and efficiently, politely answering all the officer's questions.

When Jessica apologised for being so vague about her own recollections the officer comforted her. 'That's all right, miss. It's only natural, after the shock you've had. We've got the lad, of course, thanks to Mr Hayward here. Time was when that kind of thing was only a city problem.'

It was almost ten o'clock when he left. Jessica felt exhausted. The kind of deadening exhaustion that made the senses blur and the mind and body scream silently for sleep.

After he had escorted the police officer to the door, Daniel came back, took one look at her and pronounced curtly, 'You've had enough. I should have realised and——'

'And what? Thrown him out?' Jessica asked wryly. 'Would you mind if I went to bed?' she asked him. 'If I stay down here much longer, I'll be asleep on the sofa.'

'Can I make you a bedtime drink?' Daniel offered. 'Something hot and milky and spiced with something alcoholic, as the doctor suggested?'

Jessica shook her head.

She half expected Daniel to offer to carry her upstairs. Not that she needed carrying. It was her arm that was injured, after all. But he was cosseting her as though she were something vulnerable and precious. He didn't offer, though, merely standing at the bottom of the stairs watching her until she reached the top safely.

Another man in similar circumstances might have tried to make capital out of their intimacy, and the fact that he did not confirmed all the conclusions she had already drawn about him.

The house only had one small bathroom, and it had no lock, but she felt completely at ease with the fact that, for the first time in her life, she was sharing her home with someone else. Daniel wouldn't crowd her or push...

She winced as she tried to lift her arm to remove her sweater, and found she couldn't. It would be simple enough to call downstairs to Daniel for help, but although half of her ached for the intimacy of his hands on her body, even in performing such a mundane chore as helping her overcome the problems of her sore arm, the other half wanted to draw out the sweetness of this first stage of their relationship.

By the time she got into her nightshirt and to bed she was already half-asleep, her eyes closing and her breathing deepening.

She slept soundlessly for several hours, not stirring even when the stairs creaked under Daniel's tread and he hesitated outside her door for a few seconds before going on to his own room.

The nightmare started abruptly, quickly gathering terrifying momentum, a sickening kaleidoscope of too vividly remembered terrors and fears. The darkness choked and blinded her. She moved despairingly in her sleep, feeling the sharp remembered pain of bonds breaking her skin, of fear, acrid and sour in her mouth, and a dangerous fever in her head.

She tore at the gag against her mouth and screamed out in her panic, a primitive, splintering sound that tore at her throat muscles and woke Daniel instantly.

CHAPTER FOUR

WHEN he came rushing into her room, Jessica was awake as well, sitting up in bed, hugging her arms around her shaking body, staring blindly at the wall.

'Jessica. It's all right. Everything's all right. It was just a bad dream,' he told her soothingly, summing up the situation immediately and sitting down next to her on the bed, drawing her gently against his body so that her back was resting against the warmth of his bare chest, his arms wrapping over her own.

'It's all right, now. It's all right.'

He might have been soothing a frightened child, Jessica recognised numbly as his voice penetrated the miasma of terror that waking from her nightmare had done little to disperse.

'It's OK,' he told her softly. 'You're safe. What happened this morning...'

Immediately Jessica stiffened.

'Not this morning,' she managed to whisper. Her throat ached, probably as a result of her screams, she recognised as she swallowed against the pain. She would have to tell him the truth now, otherwise he would be entitled to think her neurotic at the very least.

'Not this morning,' she repeated hoarsely. 'Something that happened...before.'

Now it was his turn to tense, and oddly she was reassured by this evidence that he was not, after all, omniscient.

'Do you want to talk about it?'

The words came slowly, almost reluctantly, and the thought crossed her mind that she might have read too much into what he had said and done, into how he had looked at her, and that he might not want to be burdened by her confidences.

Immediately she started to withdraw into her protective shell and, as though he knew exactly what she was feeling, his hold on her tightened and he said raggedly, 'I don't want to push you into giving me confidences you might later regret, confidences that might make you resent me.'

He turned her towards him, so that the top half of her body was pressed flat and hard against his bared chest. With a finger that shook slightly, he traced the shape of her half-parted mouth.

'This is crazy,' he whispered to her. 'I've never experienced anything like this before...never felt such an instant rapport with another human being. I'm afraid of demanding too much from you, of frightening you off me.'

Jessica gave a shaky laugh, wanting to tell him that that was impossible, but suddenly too shy. The sensation of his callused fingertip moving so delicately against the sensitive flesh of her lips was playing havoc with her senses. She could feel the shallow thud of his heartbeat, and knew its excitement matched the rapid beat of her own.

'You don't have to tell me anything you don't want to,' he was whispering against her ear, and the temptation to turn towards him and incite him to slide his mouth over her own and kiss her as her senses told her he could kiss her almost overwhelmed her.

But now was not the time for making love. If they did, she would never have been entirely sure that she hadn't used the potent drug of his lovemaking to alleviate the fear that still lingered in her mind.

'I want to tell you,' she whispered back, and then added truthfully, 'I *need* to tell you.'

He listened in a silence she found hard to fathom as she told him the story of the bank raid and her kidnap. Only once did she surprise emotion in his expression, and that was when she mentioned being taken to the flat and left there.

'I didn't know they'd left me on my own,' she told him, shuddering still at the memory. 'I thought they were there, watching me.'

For a moment she forgot that she was here in the present, safe in his arms, in her own bedroom, and her body went rigid with the old, remembered fear.

Daniel neither spoke nor moved, simply holding her lightly as though her body had the fragility of an eggshell, but when she eventually recovered enough to turn and look at him his eyes were burning gold with murderous rage.

'It was all a long time ago,' she told him huskily.

'But you still remember it.'

'Yes...Yes... After I was rescued...well, I was ill for quite a long time. Nervous exhaustion. Shock. And then when I did recover, I didn't feel I could ever face going back into the bank. I'd realised, you see, that all my life I'd been trying desperately to be the person my parents wanted me to be, and that that person was not necessarily the real me. I know they were disappointed. I'd grown up knowing that it was my duty to follow my father into the bank, to take the place of the brother I'd never had. So, after I'd told them of my decision, I decided it was best to...to distance myself from them a little.'

'So you don't see much of your parents, then?' Daniel asked her carefully.

Unaware that she was almost wringing her hands with anguish, she told him, 'I daren't. I feel I can't trust them not to put pressure on me to go back.'

'To go back? To the bank, do you mean?'

'Yes. It means so much to my father. They don't really understand.'

'And because of *that* you don't trust them?'

Why was he making it sound like an accusation? She looked at him, but could discern nothing hostile in the clear, calm gaze of his eyes. Even so, she shivered a little, as though she had just been exposed to a cold draught.

'Not them, nor anyone involved with them,' she admitted tightly. 'You see, my father has considerable influence. In the early days, he used some of my friends to try and manipulate me into staying in London.'

'You're making your parents sound extremely selfish and hard-hearted,' he commented quietly.

Immediately guilt filled her. 'No. They aren't . . . not really. They just think that they know what's best for me.'

'A fault common to most parents,' Daniel told her, and then said lightly, 'So I take it that if I said that *I* knew your parents, you would banish me from your life forthwith. Is that right?'

She looked at him uncertainly, unable to tell from his expression whether or not he was teasing her. Her breath locked in her throat and for a moment she couldn't speak. When she did, her voice was raw with pain.

'I'd have to, you must see that . . .' She hesitated and then asked tensely, 'You aren't trying to tell me that you *do* know my father, are you?'

She had gone cold at the thought, everything that she was feeling revealed in her eyes.

Daniel was looking at her, his eyes sombre.

She felt the breath leak from her chest.

'I don't want to talk about it any more,' she told him shakily, knowing her question was idiotic. Of course he didn't know them; she was becoming paranoid.

'I think I've spent enough time now feeling sorry for myself. I know my parents love me,' she added painfully. 'Neither of them would force me to go back, but I'm terrified that living with them, seeing my father's disappointment, would force me to give in. You see, the bank's been headed by a member of our family ever since its inception. If I don't marry and produce a son—— '

'Is that what you intend to do?' he asked her thoughtfully.

'No!' Her response was sharp and immediate. 'At least, not to provide the bank with a chairman!'

'Well, in these volatile days of mergers and take-overs, I don't suppose it will be long before your father finds himself a partner to help him to shoulder the burden of command.'

He sounded so uninterested that Jessica immediately thought she was boring him.

'I'm all right now,' she told him quickly, trying to pull away from him. 'You must be exhausted. You've been so kind, and now I've ruined your sleep.'

'It was already ruined,' he told her briefly, his eyes resting betrayingly on the swell of her breasts.

Immediately she was intensely conscious of the thinness of her satin nightshirt, so demure with its long sleeves and prim neck, but the fabric itself was anything but prim, and neither was the way it moulded itself to the soft curves of her body.

Heat began to prickle under her skin. Her body, unused to the intensity of physical desire, reacted instinctively to Daniel's maleness, and her face flushed with mortification as she realised that the wanton hardening of her nipples was clearly visible to him.

'Jessica.' He breathed her name thickly, roughly almost, as though it were a protest. Her body shook with the force of her own emotions, incited by the message she could read in his eyes.

'I want you,' he whispered achingly. 'But now isn't the right time—for either of us.'

She knew it was true, but it shocked her that he should have needed to say the words. In her second-hand experience of male to female relationships and desires, it was always the woman who called a halt, not the man—the woman who thought beyond the immediacy of the moment.

'I'm sorry,' she responded tautly, and watched mesmerised as the golden eyes turned fiercely molten and beneath his skin the bones of Daniel's face tightened.

'For what?' he demanded roughly. 'For responding to me like this?' His hand touched the curve of her breast—instant heat, instant pleasure, instant awareness of how she would feel if he were to strip her nightshirt from her and stroke first his hands and then his mouth over her rebellious skin, stormed through her. Her body didn't want to listen to warnings or common sense. Her body wanted to submerge itself eagerly in all the pleasures it sensed he could give.

'Dan...iel...'

He felt the spasm of longing convulse her body, and his hand dropped from her breast to lie flat and hard, low down on her belly, so that the heel of his palm pressed against the swell of her pubic bone and his fingers curved round her, not so much in a caress, but in a gesture that acknowledged the extent of her need and sought to comfort her for it.

That he should know so easily everything she was feeling and experiencing should have embarrassed her. After all, she was *not* familiar with the rebellious arousal of her own flesh, nor with the emotions that churned inside her, but instead of embarrassment she felt a tender, aching swell of gratitude that he should be so aware of her vulnerability and seek to comfort her in it.

'I want you,' he told her raggedly. 'I want to stay here with you now, to take you in my arms and explore every satin inch of you. I want to kiss the hollow here at the base of your throat and feel the pulse of your life's blood go crazy for me. I want to hold your breasts in the palms of my hands, to feel you arching your back in supplication of my mouth against you here.' His free hand touched the hard crown of one breast and she shuddered delicately, breathing shallowly. 'I want to hear you cry out to me in need, your body moist and fragrant with the heat of arousal.' His fingers left her breast and stroked lightly against the valley between them, while the other hand—the hand that held her so intimately, and so, she had thought, detachedly—moved briefly against her, causing her body to yield and open.

The small, frantic sound she made in her throat was as much one of panic as of desire and, as though he knew exactly what she was feeling, his hand dropped to her thigh and stayed there.

'And that's only how I want to touch and see *you*. I could spend the rest of the night telling you how you're going to make me feel when *you* touch *me*.'

He got up off the bed and stood with his back to her, but not before she had seen the tell-tale signs of his physical arousal.

Her pulse-rate doubled. She wanted to tell him to stay, but she knew he was right, that it was too soon . . . far too soon for them to become lovers.

'Will you be all right if I leave you?' he asked thickly.

Jessica nodded and managed an unsteady, 'Yes,' watching him walk to the door.

'How are you feeling this morning?'

'My arm's very bruised and stiff.' They were both standing in Jessica's kitchen. She had woken up early and had dressed and come downstairs, only to find Daniel there before her.

For the first time she felt ill at ease and nervous in his presence. In the cold, clear light of the sharply clear October morning he looked so much more formidable than she remembered, so much more male... She winced inwardly, wondering how much of a fool she must have made of herself last night. Had he really withdrawn from making love to her because he genuinely felt it was too soon, or had that simply been a polite way of saying that he didn't really want her?

As she tried to follow her normal morning routine, she deliberately avoided looking at him, jumping when he reached out and removed the teapot from her grasp as he said firmly, '*I* meant every word I said last night, but if you're having any regrets...if you're beginning to wonder if this...this thing that's happening between us isn't something you want to pursue, you don't have to be afraid of saying so.'

He watched her gravely as her face betrayed her emotions.

'You must think I'm behaving like an idiot,' she told him helplessly. 'Heavens, I'm an adult, not a child!'

'Even adults have been known to regret in the cold light of morning things that happen in the blurring, protective darkness of night,' Daniel told her. For the first time there was a trace of cynicism in his voice.

'I don't regret telling you about...about the past,' Jessica told him firmly, and then added bravely, 'and I'm not having second thoughts about...about us.' She looked at him and said with helpless honesty, 'I'm just not used to this kind of intimacy. I've never felt like this before.'

'Neither have I,' Daniel told her almost fiercely. 'There's nothing in my past... *No one*,' he emphasised, 'with whom I've experienced a tenth of what I'm feeling now.' He stopped and pushed his fingers into his hair in a gesture of baffled self-irritation. 'I don't know how to handle this, either,' he told her in a softer, muffled voice. 'One half of me says, "Don't push her...Don't rush." The other—the old male hunting instinct, I suppose—says, "Make sure of her now, before someone else snatches her away from you.'

His admission startled her, softening her defences. She hadn't given any thought to his vulnerabilities and fears; she had automatically assumed that a man so obviously very much in charge of his life and himself would never experience the kind of doubts to which she was prey.

'Look,' he said gently, coming towards her and taking hold of her hands, 'I know you're trying to tell me that you don't want to be rushed into an intimate relationship because you haven't had that kind of relationship before, and, like anything unknown, at times it appears dangerous and a little frightening. I can't claim that you'll be the first woman I've made love with, but I *can* tell you you'll be the first woman I've loved, and so intensely that I feel I hardly dare let you out of my sight in case you disappear.'

Jessica sat down and stared at him. His open declaration of love stunned her.

'But it's too soon,' she whispered protestingly. 'We haven't even known one another twenty-four hours yet.'

'I knew the moment I saw you,' Daniel told her harshly. 'You looked at me and it was as though suddenly the world had shifted into brilliant focus... as though a missing piece of my life had suddenly slotted into place... I can't explain it or rationalise it, Jessica,' he told her grimly. 'And I know quite well if someone was standing here telling me what I'm saying to you, I'd probably not believe him. There is no rational explanation for what I'm feeling. And you feel it, too. You might not want to admit it, but we both know it's true.'

'It might just be because of the raid,' Jessica argued tensely. 'Things like that unleash all kinds of strong emotions——'

'I saw you before the raid,' Daniel reminded her, his voice low and rough so that, somehow, the sound of it almost seemed to touch her skin.

She hesitated for a moment, like a diver confronted with a particularly high board, and then, taking hold of her courage, she said huskily, 'I'm frightened, Daniel... Frightened of trusting myself to what I'm feeling...frightened of giving myself to——'

'To me?' he asked her savagely, shocking her with the violence of his voice and expression. 'Don't you think I feel the same way? Don't you think anyone committing themselves to another human being knows that same fear? I can't tell you what to do, Jessica. I'm already in too deep to draw back, or to give you any detached advice. What I think you must ask yourself is what you fear the most... Is it the fact that sharing your life with me will breach your protective solitude, or is it because you fear that the relationship won't last?'

'Both,' Jessica admitted painfully. 'Especially our relationship not lasting.'

'So you're not really sure about your own feelings...about their ability to endure?'

His question trapped her. Of course she was sure about what she felt, and had been from the moment she had realised that the rapport she felt for him wasn't based on gratitude for his help and kindness, but came from what she felt for Daniel himself.

'Or is it the strength of *my* feelings you doubt?' he asked her softly, watching her as betraying colour stained her pale face. 'There's nothing I can do or say that will convince you,' he told her quietly. 'Only time can do that. I want it all, Jess. You, marriage...a family...'

He saw her tension and his mouth twisted in an ironic smile.

'All right, I know you're not ready for that kind of commitment yet.'

'I need time,' she told him helplessly. 'You're so sure...so... I want to trust how we feel, but it's all so new to me. We need time to get to know one another properly.'

'Yes,' he agreed, 'starting with today. How about coming with me when I go to see the builders you and Mrs G recommended? I need to have someone who's going to treat the restoration of the house with a bit more care and consideration than the cowboy who brought down one of the bedroom ceilings.'

'Is the house listed?' Jessica asked him.

'No, but I want to make sure the work is done sympathetically and in keeping with the period of the house. I had planned to go over to Bath this afternoon. I've got an appointment at an architectural salvage place there. They're going to look out for some of the stuff I need. Come with me, Jess. Spend the day with me. I promise I shan't pressure you. You can't work, and we both know damned well that if I leave you here, before I'm clear of the village you'll be trying to work.'

Already he seemed to know her so well, while she... Sometimes she thought she knew him, and then suddenly she would be confronted by another, unfamiliar aspect to his personality that would check her.

Spend the day with him... Why not? After all, as he had said, she couldn't work. If she stayed in the cottage on her own she would only brood, and while they were in Bath she could possibly call at the shop and discuss any new commissions they might have for her.

'I'll come with you,' she told him quickly before she could change her mind. 'I could show you where the builder has his office—it's not far from Bath.'

Instantly his whole face softened.

'Good girl,' he told her softly, and then leaned towards her as though he was going to kiss her.

A fierce thrill of anticipation ran through her body, tensing her muscles.

But then he hesitated and drew back, saying ruefully, 'No, perhaps not... I promised I wouldn't rush you, didn't I?'

Cross with herself for her own sharp feeling of disappointment, she announced that there were things she had to do before she could go out—such as feeding Cluny and getting changed into something warm enough for the gusty autumn day with its sudden sharp spirals of wind and its cold, almost frosty air—and then waited tensely for Daniel to object, as she had so often heard the husbands and lovers of friends object when they were kept waiting. Instead he said agreeably that that presented no problems since he had a couple of phone calls to make, if she would allow him the use of her phone, and additionally that it would be his chore to clear away their breakfast things since her now painfully stiff arm would necessarily mean that it would take her longer to get changed.

Surreptitiously watching him as he deftly cleared the table and started to wash up, Jessica reflected that she had seldom seen a man so at home and at ease with domestic chores. Turning round and seeing her watching him, Daniel grinned, and explained, 'Early training. Since I wasn't the girl she so desperately wanted, Ma had to make do with my help when the twins came along. I drew the line at pushing the pram,' he added, still smiling.

'You mother wanted a *girl*?' Jessica asked him curiously, puzzled. 'But, surely...?'

'What—all parents want sons? Not so,' Daniel told her, shaking his head.

'You must have found that very hard,' Jessica said slowly, remembering her own pain on discovering how much her parents had wanted a son.

Daniel frowned.

'I said that my mother wanted a girl, not that she didn't love me, Jess. There is a difference, you know.'

She opened her mouth to deny his statement, and then closed it again, knowing that it was true that, although she hadn't been the son her parents had hoped for, they did undoubtedly love her.

Once upstairs, like any woman in love, the moment she opened her wardrobe doors she discovered she didn't have a thing to wear, or, more truthfully, she didn't have anything to wear that she considered worthy of inciting Daniel's admiration.

Why was it that women were so vulnerable where their physical appearance was concerned? she wondered idly, frowning over the perfectly adequate contents of her wardrobe. Why was it that their deepest and most instinctive feelings of self-worth sprang from their public image and the way that people reacted to it?

For Daniel, she wanted to turn heads as they walked down the street... For Daniel, she wanted others to admire and maybe even envy his choice of woman a little, and yet the contents of her wardrobe were geared for her working life, and living here in the country. Warm, practical clothes designed to withstand the elements, good-quality clothes, but clothes that were scarcely worthy of the description "**glam**orous".

Just for one fleeting and revealing moment she thought regretfully of the shopping trip her mother had insisted on taking her on the last time they had met. She had refused the enticement of the expensive designer-label clothes her mother had drawn to her attention, pointing out firmly that on her income she could scarcely afford such luxuries, and that, anyway, she had no need of them.

Useless now to regret the soft pastel cashmeres, the fine, delicate silks, the thin, narrow skirts...

Instead she removed from its hanger a pleated woollen skirt in dark blue and green tartan enlivened by bright red and yellow lines.

The skirt had been an impulse buy the previous winter, from an exclusive shop in Bath. With it went a soft yellow sweater, and the sleeveless gilet which was the same dark blue as the skirt, lined with the yellow of her sweater.

The outfit was completed by a scarf, gloves and toning tights.

As she looked critically at her reflection, she wondered if she had the right personality to wear such striking colours. There was no doubt that the outfit was vibrantly colourful, and she hesitated for a moment, torn between leaving it on or changing into something plainer.

The painful ache in her arm decided her. The outfit must stay.

Almost shyly, she went back downstairs. The kitchen was immaculate, and Daniel was waiting for her, reading one of her books on tapestries.

'I hope you don't mind,' he apologised, smiling at her, 'but this caught my eye. There's a panelled room at the Court, or at least there will be if I can find enough panelling to repair the damaged sections. I had thought of using it as my study—a tapestry would look very effective against the panelling.'

'Very,' Jessica agreed and then warned, 'Providing that the panelling is of the earlier type.'

'It's early eighteenth century, or so I'm told. I'm afraid I'm not an expert on such things, which is another reason why I want to get hold of a reliable builder.' He grimaced in self-disgust. 'I thought I was too old to be taken in by a cowboy.'

'It happens all the time,' Jessica sympathised. 'When I first bought this place, I was lucky. The estate agent was a local man and he recommended this firm to me. I think you'll like him. He's got his own idiosyncrasies,' she warned, 'and works to his own time scale. He can seem a bit taciturn at first, but he does do a good job.'

Daniel hadn't said a word about her outfit, but the way he looked at her kindled that same feeling in the pit of her stomach which she had experienced the night before.

'I think we'd better make a move,' he said huskily, verbally confirming his reaction to her. 'Otherwise I might just be tempted to forget that we've agreed to take things slowly.'

Once inside the Daimler, she realised that she wasn't going to need the gilet while they were travelling. Daniel had already set the car in motion, and she struggled to remove it, hampered by the constriction of her seat-belt and the painful stiffness of her arm.

'Hang on. I'll pull up and help you,' Daniel told her, bringing the car to a halt and releasing his own seat-belt to reach across and snap hers free. 'Turn sideways, and then you should be able to slide it off,' he instructed.

Sitting with her back to him while he reached forward to gently manoeuvre the top free of her arms, she could feel the warm heat of his breath stirring her hair, raising goose-bumps on the nape of her neck.

'There...that should do it.'

Had she imagined that light, delicate kiss brushing her throat as he lifted her hair free of her collar? She shivered a little, wishing she had the experience and nature to turn round and say, 'I've changed my mind. Take me home and make love to me.'

But even if she had, it was hardly the sensible thing to do—to commit herself so rashly and so completely.

But wasn't she already committed? Wasn't she already involved? Wasn't she even now going to suffer as she had never suffered before in her life, if he left her? And that was what frightened her—that he might grow bored, or change his mind, or simply discover that he had after all mistaken his feelings, and that, while he walked away from her with no regrets, she would spend the rest of her life mourning his loss.

CHAPTER FIVE

THEY were going first to see Daniel's house, and, although she had often driven past it on her way to the main road which led to Bath and the motorway, Jessica felt a tiny thrill of excitement at the thought of going inside.

Her love affair with old buildings had first begun long before she had reached her teens, when an aunt of her mother's had invited her to spend a week's holiday with her in Cheshire and had taken her round some of the country's wonderful mediaeval and Elizabethan houses.

It wasn't the grand palaces which appealed to her so much as the smaller, more homely buildings, lived in by what in those days had been minor branches of the nobility, and the new, wealthy merchant classes who so vigorously intermarried with them.

After all, it was those merchants who had been responsible for so many of the beautiful things which had enhanced those homes: carpets, rugs, silks and velvets brought out of the East.

Daniel's house had been built when the Carolean period was at its apogee.

Inigo Jones and Christopher Wren might have been heralding in the dawn of the fashion for Palladian architecture in fashionable London, but judging from its exterior Jessica suspected, and hoped, that Daniel's house might have retained at least some of its original panelling.

In an effort to divert her senses from their intense responsiveness to him, she asked him about this as they headed for the house.

'The panelling in one of the bedrooms is virtually intact, although the original plasterwork ceiling is badly damaged, and then downstairs there's the hallway, a passage, and what at one time was the library, although most of the library shelves have been ripped out by a previous owner.

'At some stage the sitting-room and drawing-room were 'modernised', unfortunately. My apologies for the state of the drive,' he added, frowning as he turned off the main road and in through two stone gateposts, now without gates, and drove along an unkempt, rutted drive.

The trees which must once have lined the driveway no longer existed, and where once presumably there had been a smooth sweep of lawn perhaps studded by fine specimen trees, there was now an area of rough, untidy grass, so that the house was visible not just from the drive, but from the road as well.

'How much land does the house have?' Jessica asked Daniel.

'About two acres, and this piece you can see at the front is probably the only bit that resembles anything approaching a garden,' he told her ruefully.

'The whole thing has to be cleared and redesigned, but at this stage I'm trying to concentrate on getting the house properly habitable.'

'If it's in such poor condition, wouldn't it have
been wiser for you to have stayed in London until
the work's done?' Jessica asked him, repeating less
aggressively a question she had already asked.

'Wiser in some ways, perhaps, but I want to be
on hand to make sure work is progressing as it
should. I've got quite a lot of leave due to me which
I intend to use to put all the work in hand, and I
think I can oversee things much more easily from
here than from the city.'

He saw the sadness shadowing Jessica's eyes as
she studied the frontage of the house and asked
with a frown, 'What's wrong?'

His sensitivity to her moods disconcerted her; she
had deliberately kept her fellow human beings at
bay for so long that she wasn't used to people
picking up on her feelings.

'It's the house,' she told him. 'Poor thing... It
looks so neglected and unhappy.' She flushed de-
fensively when she saw that he was smiling a little.
'Houses do have feelings,' she told him crossly,
guessing that he must think her a sentimental idiot.

'Well, then, let's go inside this one and you can
reassure it and yourself as to my intentions,' Daniel
suggested, stopping the car and switching off the
engine.

Although she loved her small cottage, Jessica
couldn't help feeling slightly envious as she studied
the impressive bulk of the building. The cream stone
had weathered over the years and in places the
window mullions were either worn or missing.

'It doesn't look so bad from the front,' Daniel
told her wryly. 'Wait until you see what some idiot

did to the windows, presumably in an attempt to let in more daylight.'

As he spoke he guided her up the steps to the front door, and unlocked it. The hallway was windowless and dark until Daniel switched on the light. The solitary bulb dangling from a ceiling cord at the top of the building illuminated a good-sized rectangular room, its walls covered with linen-fold panelling which at some stage in its life had been painted black. Damp from an upstairs room was causing the varnish to peel back in one place to reveal the natural colour of the wood. The room smelled musty and uncared for. The plasterwork ceiling was cracked, with large pieces missing. Jessica gave a soft cry of protest when she looked down at the floor and saw the desecration of the once elegant parquet. A staircase led up to a galleried landing, part of which looked dangerously unsafe.

'I'm afraid most of the other rooms are much worse than this,' Daniel told her grimly, watching the expressions chase one another across her expressive face. 'Want to have a look at them?'

Jessica nodded.

It took them just over an hour to go over the house, and once they were back downstairs in the hall she could see exactly why Daniel had fallen in love with the place. She had also seen just how much work needed to be done, and as she listened to Daniel commenting determinedly and energetically about what needed to be done her admiration of him increased.

He had not taken on an easy task and, although he teased her about her indignant claim that houses had feelings, he had admitted to her that something in the house in its appalling dereliction had called out to him, and that, although half of him had said that it would be far more sensible to find a house that needed much less expensive restoration, he had not been able to resist the silent pull of the house on his senses.

'Now you see why I need a good builder,' was his final comment as they both gave one final look at the hallway.

Nodding, Jessica turned to head for the front door, and almost missed her footing on the uneven floor.

Instantly Daniel was at her side, his arm coming out to steady her, and then sliding so naturally and easily round her shoulders, drawing her into the warmth of his body, that she could find no worthwhile reason to make any move away from him as he asked her if she would like to see round the garden.

'I'd love to—if we've got time.'

'Plenty,' he assured her. 'I thought, if you were agreeable, that we'd stop for lunch on the way to Bath. I've heard there's a very nice place a couple of miles outside the city. An old manor house that's been converted into a hotel-cum-restaurant.'

Jessica thought she knew the place he meant. Somewhere she had only heard of by repute, from her more wealthy clients. She had been expecting they would have a quick snack lunch somewhere, and she couldn't help but feel flattered that Daniel should choose to take her somewhere so exclusive. Even so, she felt bound to demur, pointing out hesitantly, 'It's rather up-market, and I'm not really dressed for that kind of place.'

Instantly Daniel frowned, the look in his eyes making her flinch a little. 'It isn't your clothes I'm taking out to lunch, it's you, Jessica,' he told her roughly. 'You're the first *real* woman I've met in one hell of a long time. Clothes don't matter. People do... but if you'd rather lunch somewhere else...'

His unexpected compliment followed by his thoughtfulness touched her unbearably. She shook her head, unable to trust her voice, unprepared for the suddenness of it when Daniel abruptly stopped walking and swung her round so that they were standing breast to breast, thigh to thigh.

The warmth of his mouth moving against the coldness of her skin, touching the outer corners of her eyes with their betraying moisture before moving to her lips with a sudden, almost fierce urgency, obliterated every single atom of common sense she had ever had.

While his hands cupped her cold face and his mouth moved on hers with such piercing intensity, nothing else mattered other than that she respond to him—give herself up to him with equal intensity. When his hands moved beneath her jacket, seeking and then finding the fullness of her breasts, she gave a voluptuous sigh of pleasure against his mouth.

Hazily she was aware that if he chose now to lie her down against the crisp dying leaves and the long, untidy grass, and make love to her, she wouldn't want to do a thing to stop him.

When he didn't after all do any such thing, but instead broke the kiss, murmuring soft, regretful words against her mouth, withdrawing his hands from her body, she told herself stoically that it was just as well, that the grass would have been wet, that the wind was cold, that they could easily have been seen, while all the time her body cried fiercely in protest that none of that mattered, that it wanted him, and that it wanted him here, now, this minute.

Of course, it was impossible for her to completely conceal what she was feeling. Her face had gone pale and strained with the effort of fighting her desire.

'Are you all right?' Daniel asked her in concern, watching her, and then before she was forced to think up a fib to explain her pallor he swore softly under his breath, and apologised.

'Your arm—I forgot... Did I hurt you?'

Quickly she shook her head.

The gardens were, as Daniel had told her, overgrown and neglected to such an extent that it was impossible to imagine what they had once been.

'One of the local libraries might have some kind of archive material that might give you some clues,' Jessica suggested thoughtfully, listening to Daniel disclosing his concern about how to best deal with the problem of redesigning the garden. 'And, of course, there are books which give quite detailed illustrations and descriptions of period gardens from which perhaps you could establish a new design.'

Dreamily she studied the untidy, dying meadow grass and stubby saplings, seeing in their place hedges of dark green yew leading the eye down tantalising vistas into walks that hinted at secret, hidden arbours. She shivered, recognising how dangerously involved with Daniel she had already allowed herself to become—to such an extent that she could easily slip into thinking of this house as her own...this garden...

Daniel saw her shiver and, mistaking its cause, said firmly, 'Come on. You're getting cold—my fault for keeping you out here so long. Let's go and have some lunch.'

Half an hour later, still protesting that a sandwich and a cup of coffee would suit her admirably, Jessica found her arm being taken in a firm grasp as Daniel led her across the immaculate gravel forecourt of the small country hotel.

This was a house of much later period than his— early Victorian, Jessica guessed from its solid appearance. It had grounds of several acres, and a classic drive set between mature trees. Even from outside it was obvious that every conceivable care and thought had been lavished on its refurbishment and maintenance, and yet she found herself thinking loyally that she preferred Daniel's house in all its decay and decrepitude.

The restaurant was pleasantly busy, but they were lucky enough to get a table.

Daniel suggested that Jessica might like a pre-lunch drink, but she saw that he himself ordered only spa water, explaining that since he was driving he preferred to keep a clear head.

Mentally Jessica applauded him. She had known too many high-flying businessmen who seemed to believe that the country's drink-drive laws did not apply to them.

The hotel specialised in fresh food of the highest quality, served with light, delicate sauces that did not overwhelm or destroy its flavour. Jessica, who ordered salmon, discovered that the sauce served with it was one of the most piquant and delicate she had ever enjoyed.

Like Daniel she refused a pudding, enjoying instead the richly flavoured coffee and a piece of fruit.

Although Jessica had expostulated that she could find her own way from the architectural salvage firm's headquarters, where Daniel had his appointment, to the shop where they sold her tapestries, Daniel insisted on accompanying her there, and Jessica noticed the way her friend's eyes quickened with interest when they both walked into her small, pretty shop.

Very few women would be indifferent to Daniel's physical appearance, she suspected as she performed the necessary introductions.

Laura Grey had started her small interior design business four years ago, slowly building on her excellent reputation, careful not to allow the business to grow so quickly that she lost control of it, and thus of the quality of the work they did.

Now the cognoscenti considered her to be one of Bath's best interior designers, possessing as she did that happy blend of innovation plus sympathetic understanding of her clients' desire to have their own input into the finished appearance of their homes.

Discreetly she waited until Daniel had left before pouncing on Jessica and demanding to know, 'Where did you find him, you lucky thing?'

Tersely Jessica explained what had happened. It shocked her that she should feel this reluctance to discuss it with her friend.

She had met Laura shortly after she moved to the village, and liked her very much indeed. If pressed, she would have admitted that she was as close to Laura as she was ever likely to allow herself to get to anyone. She admired the other girl's business flair and respected and valued her judgement, and yet now, with Laura discussing Daniel's good looks with such obvious relish and sexual curiosity, she was conscious of a sharp pang of resentment coloured with a strong desire to let Laura know in no uncertain terms that Daniel was out of bounds, both as a subject of conversation and as a man.

Uncomfortable with her own feelings, she cut across Laura's flow of enthusiasm and said almost sharply, 'I only came in to see if you'd received the Thomson order safely.'

Laura paused, eyed her thoughtfully, and then said calmly, 'Yes. It came this morning. It's lovely, and I know the Thomsons will be thrilled with it. I'm taking it out to them tomorrow.' She paused, and then said frankly, 'You can tell me to mind my own business if you wish, Jess, but am I to take it that Daniel Hayward is someone special?'

Someone special... Jessica felt her heart race with a mixture of panic and happiness.

Half of her, the old cautious, protective half, was strongly inclined to deny the suggestion, but the other half, the new, feminine, joyful side of her personality that had suddenly flowered inside her, said recklessly, 'Yes... Yes, he is.'

Laura chuckled and then teased, 'There now, that wasn't so difficult to say, was it? I must say I'm impressed. All this time we've known one another there's never been a man in your life, and you've made it plain that that's the way you wanted things, and now you turn up with Daniel in tow, with such an obvious metamorphosis having taken place.' She laughed, her eyes twinkling. 'Mind you, I can't say I'm surprised. He is rather gorgeous. What was he doing in Little Parvham, anyway? Just passing through?'

'No. He's bought a house there.' Briefly Jessica explained the situation, and added generously, 'I don't know what he intends to do with the interior of the house once all the renovations have been completed, but if he does want an interior designer I'll recommend you to him.'

'He won't need me,' Laura told her, equally generously. 'You know far more about houses of that period than I do, Jess. You're an expert in the fabrics of that era—crewelwork, tapestries...'

'Not all of the rooms are true to the original period of the house,' Jessica told her. 'And I've no idea whether Daniel intends to restore the whole of the house to its original state. The drawing-room, sitting-room and dining-room have all been remodelled several times; the last remodelling evidently took place during the fifties,' she added ruefully, 'and involved the most deplorable modernisation of the windows, and a hideously unsuitable lowering of the ceiling height which has totally ruined the proportions of the rooms. All the original fireplaces have gone. There's some serious damp damage upstairs.' She gave a brief shrug. 'Daniel has an appointment with the builder who worked on the cottage for me. He's hoping he'll agree to undertake the restoration work.'

'Mmm ... speaking of which, I was visiting a potential client today and she showed me the most marvellous old tapestry which has been in her family for umpteen generations. It's very badly worn in places, and I told her I'd have a word with you, and perhaps make an appointment for you to see it, to see whether you can repair it. I've sold nearly all the cushions you did, by the way, and if you could see your way to letting me have a fresh supply for Christmas ...

'I also think it's time you were thinking about putting up your prices. Your stuff is ridiculously cheap, you know. I was in London last week, looking at things nowhere near the quality of your work, and the price——'

'Bath isn't London,' Jessica pointed out.

'Maybe not, but with the influx of people from the city ...'

'I'll think about it,' Jessica promised her, and they were arguing amiably over the matter when the shop bell rang and Daniel walked in.

Her heart lifted at the sight of him as Jessica turned round and saw him. He was smiling at her, looking at her, as though he wanted to draw into himself the sight of her, his glance lingering for a moment on her mouth before he turned to make polite conversation with Laura, who was asking what progress he had made with the salvage company.

'Excellent. They think they may be able to match the panelling in the library, and provide fireplaces for most of the rooms. I fell in love with a staircase they've got there. It's after the school of Grinling Gibbons,' he told Jessica, 'but I'd like you to see it before I commit myself.'

The staircase in the house was badly damaged and abominable anyway, but it wasn't the thought of replacing it with something far more suitable that was making her pulse race so ecstatically, it was the look Daniel was giving her, the way he was consulting her, including her, making an open statement about her place in his life, and so naturally, so easily that she might always have been there. As easily and naturally as he slipped his arm around her as they left the shop, drawing her against his side, solicitous about her bruised arm, eager to hear how she had got on with Laura, and genuinely pleased for her when she passed on Laura's flattering comments about the standard and appeal of her work.

'Perhaps I ought to commission you now for a tapestry for the library,' he teased her. I might not be able to afford you once you put up your prices and your work becomes the "in" thing.'

Jessica shook her head. 'I won't allow that to happen,' she told him firmly. 'I love my work, and it's always a pleasure to work for people who share my love of it. The last thing I want is for my tapestries to become a fashion fad. Shown off today, like a new designer frock, and then thrown to the bottom of a cupboard tomorrow, because it's no longer the "in" thing. Just as long as I can earn a reasonable living, I'm content.'

He had stopped walking and she, perforce, had to stop as well. He turned to look at her, a grave, searching look that made her quiver inwardly.

'I love you, Jessica,' he told her quietly.

The middle of a windy, busy Bath thoroughfare was the very last place she had ever imagined receiving a declaration of love, but as she stood gazing back at him Jessica discovered that it wasn't the place that mattered, but the words and the man who said them.

A fervent response trembled on her lips, but she was too shy to make it, too unsure still—not of her feelings, or even really of his, but of trusting that this happiness could last, as though in some way she doubted her worthiness to be the recipient of such pleasure, like a child receiving the munificence of a longed-for and wholly unexpected Christmas gift of such magnitude that it feared the gift had really been intended for someone else.

'The builder,' she said shakily. 'We're going to be late.'

Was it disappointment that darkened his eyes, or irritation? His arm was still around her, but she couldn't be sure.

She heard him sigh, and then he said quietly, 'You're right. Come on, then. Can you direct me there?' he asked her as he opened the car door for her.

'Yes,' Jessica assured him. 'It isn't very far. Just a couple of miles outside the city centre.'

The builder ran his business from a small yard with an office attached to it. The building had originally been part of the stable block attached to a large Georgian house, and the sympathetic way the restoration work had been carried out was an excellent advertisement for his skills.

Jessica waited patiently as Daniel paused to inspect the stonework. The yard was a fascinating place. The builder was also involved in a small way in architectural salvage, though nowhere near as large or as well known as the company Daniel had visited earlier, and her eye was caught by some iron railings which she paused to admire as she waited for Daniel.

'These windows are very much the sort of thing I want for the house,' Daniel told her, pointing out the stone-mullioned windows to the building.

'They're new ones,' Jessica informed him. 'Alan Pierce employs a stonemason.'

She had offered to wait in the car while Daniel saw the builder, but to her pleasure he had insisted on her joining them.

He had talked of loving her, and, for her, love—real love—went hand in hand with permanency, marriage, children...but did loving someone mean the same thing to him? He had indicated that it did, but caution warned her not to take too much for granted. Life had made her wary, reluctant to trust her own emotions and judgements.

Daniel said he loved her; she certainly knew that she loved him, but somewhere deep down inside there were shadows...doubts. Was it because she had never considered herself to be the kind of person to look at a stranger and know instantly and irrevocably that she loved him? Was it because she had always had the vague idea at the back of her mind that love, when and if it ever came into her life, would grow from a relationship which was already well established, and not be this sudden, lightning thing, striking into her between one heartbeat and the next? Or was it because the feelings Daniel caused within her were so alien to her normal wary, controlled approach to life that she was half resentful of them—resentful and just a little afraid?

CHAPTER SIX

DANIEL'S meeting with the builder went well enough for the two of them to be able to agree that, once he had looked at the house and confirmed that the plans drawn up by Daniel's architect were compatible with the capabilities of his workforce, he would be able to start work almost immediately.

When Daniel looked surprised and pleased he went on to explain that under normal circumstances it would have been weeks, if not months, before he would have been able to do the work, but a barn conversion on which he had been due to start work had hit some last-minute snags, which meant a long delay while work went back to the planning stage.

Having made an appointment to meet the builder at the house in the morning, they set off back for the village.

Although she didn't say anything, Jessica's arm and shoulder were beginning to ache quite painfully. She thought she had done a very good job of hiding this fact from Daniel, until he pulled up in front of her cottage and said abruptly, 'I'm sorry. I've exhausted you. Thoughtless of me.'

He sounded so terse that Jessica felt for a moment that her weakness irritated him. Her father had always been rather intolerant of anyone less than physically one hundred per cent. It was his boast that he never caught so much as a cold, and that he had never in all his working life had to have time off through ill health, and so she said quickly, 'I'm not normally like this. I'm pretty tough really.'

As though he sensed the vulnerability and defensiveness hidden by her quick smile and light voice, Daniel caught hold of her good arm, sliding his hand down it. His fingers brushed the turbulent pulse, the delicate inner skin of her wrist, sending her pulse-rate into turbulent disorder. He turned her hand over, studying her palm so intently that she started to tremble, and then he lifted her hand to his mouth, dropping a light kiss into her palm.

'I wasn't criticising you, Jess,' he told her softly. 'I was condemning myself for being thoughtless.'

She looked at him, her breath catching on a ragged sigh as he read the emotions chasing one another across her face.

'Jess... Jess...' he said rawly, lifting her palm to his lips a second time, but this time their pressure was hard and forceful, and when she quivered under the assault of sensations rioting through her his tongue caressed the soft pads of flesh at the base of her fingers. When they curled in immediate reaction to the rush of pleasure swamping her, he bit gently into the soft mound at the base of her thumb, and then less gently, so that she shuddered violently, her eyes huge and dark with bewilderment.

'Don't look at me like that,' he muttered roughly, his thumb registering the too rapid thud of her pulse, his eyes monitoring the hectic flush staining her cheekbones, his body responding violently to her arousal.

'Why?'

Her lips parted softly on the question, a tiny frown etched between her eyebrows.

'Because it makes me want to do this.'

His hand cupped her head, sliding into her hair, his fingers hard and warm against her scalp. During the day his jaw had darkened with the new growth of beard, and when he kissed her the roughness of his skin against the softness of her own created a *frisson* of sharp pleasure that made her shiver inside and break out in a rash of goose-flesh outside.

She had never done anything like this before— never been kissed so passionately and demandingly in full sight of anyone who chose to walk past the car, and been so oblivious to that fact that if Daniel had started to undress her all she would have known was that now, at last, she was going to feel the delirious joy of his touch against her skin.

It was a car backfiring in the distance that brought her to her senses, making her pull back from him, her eyes still cloudy and confused by the suddenness and intensity of her own desire.

Neither of them spoke as they went inside, but Jessica was acutely aware of Daniel's hand on her arm, of the tension gripping him—the same tension that was still invading her. She sensed his impatience, his male desire to carry them both to the culmination of the feelings they had just shared.

They looked at one another in silence, but the air between them quivered with expectancy and anticipation. If she went towards him now, if she touched him, spoke to him, Jessica knew that he would make love to her. She wanted him to so intensely, her need so sharp and spearing, that it seemed incredible to imagine that she had ever hesitated or doubted. The Jessica who she was now, this moment, looked back in incredulous amazement at the Jessica she had been, unable to comprehend why she had had such doubts, such fears.

And then the phone rang, the sound shrill and imperious, fragmenting the fragile bubble of desire that held them both captive. Jessica reached for it instinctively, her voice unsteady and slightly higher-pitched than usual as she said her name.

'Jessica, darling, are you all right? I've been trying to reach you all day.'

'Mother... Is something wrong?'

Discreetly Daniel moved out of earshot to give her privacy, but there was nothing private she wanted to say to her mother. Strange that, while she loved her and knew that she was loved in turn, there were still these immense barriers between them.

'No, nothing's wrong. It's just that it's rather a long time since I spoke to you.'

Instantly Jessica felt guilty, uncomfortably aware of the low tone of unhappiness in her mother's voice.

Jessica suppressed her guilt.

'Are you sure you're all right, darling?' her mother pressed. 'You don't sound your normal self. Your father and I worry about you, living alone.'

'Living in London is much more dangerous,' Jessica pointed out wryly, and then, aware of the quality of her mother's silence, mentally cursed herself. No doubt her mother thought she was making an unkind reference to her kidnapping.

'Why don't you come home for the weekend?'

Jessica felt her stomach knotting as it always did at the thought of spending time with her parents, of being vulnerable to their subtle persuasion and coercion, and yet she heard the yearning note beneath the lightness of her mother's words.

'I can't, Mother,' she fibbed, hating herself for her own weakness. 'I'm afraid I've already got something on.'

'A date?' her mother enquired, her voice brightening.

A date... What would her parents say if they knew about Daniel? If they knew she had fallen in love? Not that she was going to tell them. Not yet. Not until she herself was sure.

Sure of what? Of Daniel? Of herself? As she muttered something non-committal and replaced the receiver the euphoria of her earlier mood of reckless certainty and confidence had gone, replaced by one of uncertainty and tension.

Daniel obviously sensed it. He gave her a thoughtful look and offered quietly. 'If you'd like me to leave...'

She shook her head. Part of her did. Part of her wanted to crawl back into the security of the solitary life with which she was so familiar, but another part of her wanted to break free of the old Jessica and her fears.

'No,' she said huskily. 'Please stay.'

And as they looked at one another across the width of the room she wondered if he realised that those were probably the most portentous words she had ever said.

As though he knew what she was going through, over the meal, which he had insisted on preparing, Daniel deliberately kept the conversation light and general.

He was interesting to talk with—not like some men, whose entire lives and interests were themselves and their careers. Daniel was widely read, and knowledgeable, drawing her out to talk about herself so easily and gently that she scarcely realised what he was doing.

At nine o'clock exhaustion suddenly hit her.

'You're tired,' Daniel said quietly. 'I'd better go.'

Go? Jessica stared at him. She had taken it for granted that he would be staying the night again.

He touched her face with his hand, his touch both reassuring and tender.

'I promised I wouldn't rush you,' he reminded her. 'But if I stay here with you tonight, I may not be able to keep that promise. We both know that.' He frowned and hesitated. 'I want your love *and* your trust, Jessica.'

She desperately wanted to beg him to stay, to push caution aside and say that she had changed her mind, that she was ready now to make the fullest kind of commitment to him, but the words stuck in her throat, a paralysing shyness silencing her, and by the time she had found her voice he was already on his feet and walking towards the door.

'I'll get my bag,' he told her quietly, and then added, 'Tomorrow, would it be too much if I asked you to be with me when Alan Pierce comes to go round the house? I'd like your views on anything he has to say.'

'A woman's touch,' Jessica said lightly, trying to mask her pleasure that he should want her there.

'No,' he corrected, watching her. '*The* woman's touch.'

He wouldn't let her go with him to the car, saying that it was too cold outside. He brushed his lips fleetingly against her forehead before firmly stepping back from her.

'Nine o'clock tomorrow?' he suggested.

Jessica nodded, and then offered almost shyly, 'If you want to make it a bit earlier, we could have breakfast together.'

'I'd like that, Jess.' He seemed about to say something else, but then stopped and opened the door.

The house felt empty without him, and yet, after all, she had only known him a couple of days.

Tiredly she went upstairs, wishing she had had the courage to ask him to stay, and yet admitting ruefully later, when she studied herself in the full-length mirror in her bathroom, that her bruised arm and shoulder, all swollen and now vividly coloured, purple and blue, were hardly appealing.

Morning brought an end to the brief interlude of blue skies and bright autumn sunshine. The wind had picked up during the night, blowing in pewter rainclouds and turning the whole landscape a dull, leaden grey.

Lethargically Jessica surveyed the contents of her cupboard and wondered what on earth she was going to give Daniel for breakfast. A trip to the local market town to stock up at the supermarket there was plainly called for, but she couldn't summon any enthusiasm for such an undertaking. She hated supermarket shopping at the best of times, and could never visit one without wondering how on earth mothers with under-school-age children managed. The old-fashioned corner-type shops might not have sold the wide range of goods supplied by supermarkets, but they had a friendliness, a warmth that was lacking from these huge soulless buildings. The worst time for shopping in them, as far as she was concerned, was early in the evenings or at weekends, when all the other shoppers seemed to be in family groups and she felt as though she was the only person there who was on her own.

She wondered curiously how Daniel lived, where he did his shopping. As a successful businessman no doubt he ate out a lot. Daniel... Was every path her thoughts took these days destined to lead her back to him? Was she already so dangerously involved with him that she couldn't, didn't *want* to focus on anything or anyone else?

As she closed the fridge door she glanced upwards towards the window, sighing as she saw the rain spattering against the glass, and then she remembered that tucked away in one of her top cupboards was an unopened packet of porridge bought on impulse one bitterly cold spring day and left unopened all summer.

She wasn't tall enough to reach the top cupboards in the kitchen without standing on a stool, but she had forgotten the weakness in her arm, and as she stood on the stool and lifted her arm to open the cupboard her bruised muscles protested, and the pain in them made her cry out in surprise and almost lose her balance.

'Jessica! What the devil...?'

The sight of Daniel standing in her kitchen, glowering at her while he set down the paper bags he was carrying and came quickly towards her, made her tremble so much that the stool wobbled even more. The floor was uneven and the stool not the safest thing to stand on, she knew, but her situation was surely hardly perilous enough to warrant either the grim look Daniel was giving her or the stifled curse he muttered under his breath as he crossed the kitchen and unceremoniously lifted her off the stool.

Once her feet were touching the floor, though, he didn't let her go.

She could feel the heavy thud of his heart through her thin sweater.

The heat from his body lapped her in a warmth which was rapidly making her own flesh burn. It was hard to keep her voice calm and steady as she asked, 'What did you do that for? I was perfectly safe.'

'Safe? Your front door was unlocked and open when I heard you cry out.'

The grimness was beginning to leave his mouth, and guiltily Jessica remembered that she *hadn't* checked that the door was closed and locked after she took the milk in.

'I forgot about my arm,' she told him breathlessly. 'That was why I cried out.'

'Idiot!' Daniel told her roughly. 'Don't you *know* that the majority of patients in Britain's out-patients' hospital departments go there through accidents caused in the home? What was it you wanted, anyway? I'll get it for you.'

She told him, and then explained about her near-empty fridge and her concern over what she was going to give him to eat.

'I've brought our breakfast with me,' he told her wryly, watching her nose twitch appreciatively as she focused on the carrier bags he had put down on the table. The unmistakable smell of freshly baked bread reached her, making her mouth water.

'You've been into Long Eaton,' she accused him. 'You must have been. That's the only place around here where they have a bakery.'

'I was awake early,' he told her. 'Mrs G had mentioned the bakery, and so I thought I'd drive over and see what they had to offer.'

'They make the most wonderful croissants,' Jessica began with regret. 'They use French flour and a special recipe...' Her voice trailed away, her eyes rounding with pleasure as Daniel delved into one of the carrier bags and told her,

'I bought some, and some of Mrs Neville's cousin Ann's very special blackcurrant conserve,' he added virtuously.

Jessica started to laugh, happiness rising inside her like effervescent bubbles, intoxicating her. She wanted to fling her arms around him and tell him how wonderful he was, but because by nature she was cautious and unused to expressing her feelings, she said mock severely instead, 'That conserve is wickedly expensive, and loaded down with calories.'

'Mrs Neville told me it's your favourite.'

It was the way he was looking at her, and not the words, that silenced her—the knowledge that he cared.

She reached out to touch him, her hand trembling a little as her fingertips found the hard line of his jaw.

'It is,' she said huskily.

And then she was in his arms and he was holding her, touching her, kissing her as she had ached for him to do every time she woke up during the night and discovered that he wasn't there.

'Much more of this and I'm going to start forgetting that I promised not to rush you,' Daniel whispered thickly against her ear, stroking the soft skin of her throat with fingers that trembled betrayingly. 'And I still haven't...'

She ached to tell him that she had changed her mind, that there was nothing she wanted more than to commit herself to him completely, but instead said softly, 'Haven't what?'

'Jess, about your parents...'

'No, please, I don't want to talk about them. I know you mean well, Daniel, but it's just that I can't trust them. We'll be late for the builder,' she reminded him jerkily.

She saw him look at her, an odd expression in his eyes, composed of wryness and something that was almost pain.

'Posting No Trespassing signs, Jess?' he said drily.

The builder arrived at Daniel's house just as they were getting out of Daniel's car. He showed no surprise at seeing Jessica with Daniel, and together the three of them set off on a tour of inspection.

It took them almost three hours, with Alan Pierce making copious notes.

He listened while Daniel explained exactly what he wanted to achieve, firmly agreeing with him when Daniel said that he wanted to use salvaged materials of the right period as much as possible, resorting to new only when there was no alternative available.

The builder, as Jessica already knew, had been apprenticed as a teenager to a small family firm of craftsmen working in and around Bath, so that unlike many modern builders he was fully conversant with many of the traditional forms of building, but, listening to him discussing the work with Daniel, what surprised her was Daniel's own expertise.

When she commented on it later when the builder had gone, he told her ruefully, 'It's only information culled second-hand from books and magazine articles, I'm afraid. Unfortunately I have no practical expertise. I've always been interested in architecture and old buildings. In fact, as a teenager I had dreams of qualifying as an architect.'

Jessica looked at him in surprise.

'Did you? What made you turn to the City instead?'

He gave a brief shrug. It was cold outside in the overgrown gardens, but he was standing so that he sheltered her from the worst of the wind. There was something intensely pleasurable about standing here with him, Jessica thought as she looked up into his face, waiting for his reply.

This morning he was dressed casually in a pair of faded jeans, a woollen shirt and a rather battered and very soft leather blouson jacket, and, watching him as he had enthusiastically and knowledgeably inspected rotting pieces of wood, crumbling stonework and plaster, as comfortably at home among the dirt and mess of the old house as the builder, she hadn't been able to help contrasting him with the other men she had occasionally dated—men introduced to her via her parents, men who dressed in expensive suits and who would never in this world have dreamed of crouching down on rotting floorboards to admire the workmanship in a piece of wainscoting.

He seemed to hesitate before responding to her question, causing Jessica to frown as she saw the faint shadows darkening his eyes.

'Necessity,' he told her at last, and then leavened the starkness of the word with its undertones of past unhappiness with a wry smile. 'I don't regret it now. I find the world of finance intensely fascinating and seem to have discovered my *métier* there.'

Jessica wondered if he would go on to explain in more detail, but hesitated to press him, not wanting to intrude on memories he might prefer to keep private. His hand on her shoulder guided her along a disused and overgrown footpath, and he stopped to examine a broken stone urn which looked as though it should have been one of a pair. It guarded a set of stone steps which led down to what must once have been a south-facing lawn surrounded by herbaceous borders and enclosed by a traditional yew hedge. Now all that remained was a tangled mess. The yew hedge had reached proportions that threw ominous shadows more suitable for a graveyard than a garden. Idly, Jessica used her imagination to project a mental picture of what it might once have been, believing the subject of Daniel's past closed, and then to her surprise he said abruptly, 'Do you mind if we walk for a few minutes? I find it easier to talk that way.'

She wanted to tell him that she didn't mind what she did as long as she did it with him, but such extravagant teenage idolatry was something she felt it wiser to suppress, and so instead she shook her head, allowing him to draw her closer against his side and to keep her there as he matched his pace to hers.

'You already know something of my background,' he told her. 'What I didn't tell you was that when I was sixteen my mother's sister and her husband were killed in a car crash. They had three children, all of them under seven; the youngest, Gemma, was only eighteen months old. My aunt and uncle were only relatively young. They hadn't been able to make any financial provision for the children in the event of their deaths.

'My parents made the decision to take responsibility for them and to bring them up as they had done us. I was taking my O levels at the time. In my imagination, I'd already decided on my future: university, including training with a firm of high-ranking architects. I didn't just want to be any architect. I wanted to be articled to the best there was. I wanted to travel—Italy, Greece, the old world and then the new, to learn all that was best in my field. My father had to explain to me that, with the added responsibility of three more children, it just wasn't going to be possible for him to finance me in the way that we'd planned; architecture is a seven-year course, you see.

'Of course, I could have gone ahead with my plans, worked my own way through university, got my degree and then built up my skill and reputation. It would just have taken a bit longer, because I wouldn't have been able to devote all my time to studying. But in those days I believed less in the value of ability and the will to succeed, and far more than I should have done in my right to an unhindered education.'

'But it's not too late,' Jessica counselled quickly, remembering her own misery when compelled by duty and love to try and turn herself into the person she believed her parents wanted her to be. He could still qualify, set up in practice...

'I no longer want to,' Daniel told her, and added, 'You're missing the point, which is that I wanted my success to be handed to me, that I believed I had a *right* to expect my parents to make it possible for me to succeed. I wanted to be an architect because it seemed to me to be a glamorous, potentially high-profile life-style. My love of design and buildings came second to my love of self.'

'It must have been hard for you,' Jessica murmured. 'To have all your hopes and plans dashed like that . . .'

'Maybe, but it taught me a great deal, and I like to think that I'm a better person from what I learned. You see, initially I behaved extremely badly—in the ways that only a spoiled teenager can behave badly. I let my schoolwork slide. I sulked and complained and generally made life unpleasant all round, culminating with the failure of my A levels. I was at a private school, and fully expected my father to pay for an extra year's schooling so that I could resit them. I hoped through my bad behaviour to pressure him into financing my career as an architect—and I deliberately blinded myself to the fact that, in financing that, he would have to deprive my cousins of the same kind of education he had given us. It came as a grim shock when he told me that, far from paying for an extra year's schooling for me and wasting several more thousands of pounds, he was going to use the money instead for my cousins' education, considering that they deserved it far more than I did.

'At first I thought he was simply making an idle threat. As the eldest, despite the fact that both my parents ensured that I took my turn with chores at home, I had somehow or other during my growing-up process collected the chauvinistic belief that as a son, and the eldest child, my needs and desires somehow ranked higher than those of my siblings and cousins. My father very quickly dispatched this error.

'Instead of going on to university, I had to leave school and find myself a job.'

He saw her face and smiled.

'It wasn't as harsh as you seem to think, and taught me several salutory lessons, through which I discovered my flair for matters fiscal. I also discovered how much more self-appreciation one's achievements bring when one has earned them for oneself.

'I had to go to night-school to get the qualifications to enable me to go on to university, and by that time I had discovered my hitherto unsuspected skill with figures, so I opted to take a degree in economics.'

'And your parents?' Jessica questioned.

'Unfairly proud of my achievements, so the others tell me. The youngest of my cousins is now sitting her A levels. Like my father and sister, she wants to go into medicine. She's utterly dedicated to the ideal of doing all that she can to work for the improvement of world health, especially in the Third World countries. When I think that through my selfishness I might have deprived her of the opportunity to fulfil that ideal, I can only thank God that my parents were wise enough and loving enough to stand firm with me. That's why...'

He stopped walking and turned to face her.

'Jessica, I have to tell you,' he began earnestly, frowning as he looked down at her, his eyes shadowed and dark so that suddenly her heart missed a beat, her mind already braced as though for a blow, already anticipating that he was about to tell her something she wasn't going to like, and then before he could speak they both heard something travelling along the drive.

Daniel cursed and released her.

'That will be my ex-builder. I told him to meet me here so that I could pay him off and make it clear to him just what I think of his shoddy workmanship. I think it might be an idea if you wait for me here,' he added purposefully. 'I suspect this isn't going to be pleasant.'

He was gone for just over half an hour, and when he returned he looked so grim and remote that Jessica found it impossible to ask him what it was he had been about to say to her when they were interrupted.

CHAPTER SEVEN

Two days later, prowling edgily around her workroom, Jessica acknowledged how much she was missing Daniel.

He had had to go to London the previous morning, and wouldn't be back until this evening, and already his absence was eating into her like a canker.

Her phone rang and she raced to answer it, subduing her disappointment when it was not Daniel on the other end of the line.

In fact it was someone from the National Trust, with which she had had dealings before, wanting to make arrangements for her to travel up to Northumberland to look at and potentially do some repair work on a tapestry so fragile that it had to be worked on *in situ*.

Jessica knew the tapestry, having been asked to inspect it on a previous visit. Her discussion with Jane Robertson, who was in charge of that section of the National Trust's restoration department, was a long one. She agreed to travel up to Northumberland and to stay there overnight so that she could make a thorough study of and report on the tapestry.

'We can put you up in the house itself,' Jane told her. 'We've got a couple of rooms which we keep for visitors. One of them has the most marvellous parcel-gilt four-poster bed. It's been restored, of course, and we've had new silk hangings woven. It's terribly romantic.'

Listening to Jane enthusing about the bed and its restoration, Jessica wondered wistfully if it would be possible for Daniel to go north with her. She tried not to allow herself to be tempted by images of the two of them sharing the watery bluey-green intimacy of the silk-hung bed. When she eventually replaced the receiver her palms were damp and her heart was pounding. She was so shockingly aroused by the power of her own thoughts that she knew if he were to walk into the house now...

As though deliberately on cue, someone rang the front door bell. The shock of it pierced her, sending a tiny message of excitement-cum-panic thrilling through her.

She positively raced downstairs, flinging open the front door, her face flushed and her eyes fever-bright with anticipation.

Only it wasn't Daniel who was standing there. It was Emma. She stared at her cousin, her smile dying, to be replaced by bitter disappointment.

'Emma,' she said dully, standing to one side so that her cousin could come in. 'What brings you here?'

Her cousin, as always, was dressed in the very latest designer-label fashion, her face perfectly made-up and her hair immaculate.

She raised her eyebrows as she stalked in—no other word could adequately describe the hauteur

with which she moved, the very definite 'look at
me' aura she deliberately invoked.

'A duty visit to my godmama.' She pulled a face.
'I thought I might as well call in and see you on
my way back,' Emma told her smoothly. 'You don't
look very pleased to see me, though. Perhaps you
were expecting someone else,' she added archly as
she followed Jessica into the kitchen-cum-living-
room, grimacing faintly as she did so, and saying,
'Honestly, Jess. I can't understand how you can
live somewhere like this. It's so small and ordinary.
When I think of Uncle James and Aunt Harriet's
house in Kensington...'

She gave a delicate shudder and then turned to
Jessica, giving her one of her brilliantly unkind
smiles, so that Jessica felt her toes curling in anticipation of one of Emma's more cruelly acid jibes.

'Still, it won't be for very long, will it?' Emma
said softly. 'Aunt H. is cock-a-hoop about the
whole thing. A summer wedding next year—just
nice time to get everything organised. I expect the
engagement will be announced at the usual family
Christmas shindig. Quite a feather in your parents'
cap. And, of course, so clever of darling Uncle
James to keep it all in the family, so to speak. I
must say, though, that I *was* surprised.'

Eyebrows raised, mouth pursed, eyes cold as
winter ice, she turned to Jessica and said sweetly,
'Do you know, darling, I always thought that *if*
you did get married, it would be someone frightfully worthy and intellectual. I never imagined for
one moment that you'd fall in so easily with your
parents' plans. Not after all the fuss you made when

you decided to leave the bank. Of course, your father had to put a brave face on it at the time, and I know the whole family were rather miffed when he didn't take Cousin John's Paul into the bank in your place, but then I suppose he's always had something like this in mind. Finding himself an ambitious man, clever enough to take into the bank as a partner, and ambitious enough to actually accept such an archaic condition. It's all so frightfully Victorian, isn't it? And I suppose I shouldn't be all that surprised about Daniel's decision to go along with your father's plans. After all, he is frightfully hard-edged and ambitious, and he's never made any secret of the fact that money is very important to him, but you... well, my dear, *you* have surprised me,' Emma told her, folding herself elegantly into a chair and crossing her legs so that she could admire the silken elegance of their slenderness.

A smile of pure catlike pleasure curled her mouth as she removed one of her leather gauntlet-style gloves and drew her slender, long-nailed fingers along one slim calf.

'There's always something about black silk stockings, don't you think?' she said to Jessica and then smiled again. 'Oh, but then I forgot, since you became so independent and bucolic I don't suppose your budget stretches to such luxuries. Personally I'd rather die than wear those appalling nylon things you see so many people wearing—even with quite good clothes. You can't imagine the number of people who simply have no idea of real style.' She raised her head and studied Jessica's paper-white face with apparent surprise.

'Jess...what on earth's wrong? Have I said something I shouldn't? I must say I was surprised when I heard the news, but I didn't think you'd react like this to my knowing. Heavens, Uncle and Aunt seemed delighted. Uncle James opened a bottle of champagne when Daniel told him, and not just any champagne either. Vintage and absolutely delicious.'

Her small pink tongue touched her heavily glossed mouth as though remembering the taste of that very expensive champagne.

Something moved sluggishly and sickly in the pit of Jessica's stomach. She wanted to scream at her cousin to go away and leave her—leave her to come to terms with what she had just learned, leave her to rationalise all the disjointed information Emma had just given her—but Emma wasn't waiting for her reply, she was pouting and saying with a frown, 'And to think *I* was the one who introduced Daniel to your father.'

'*You* know Daniel?'

Jessica wasn't aware of speaking the words until she heard them resounding hollowly and painfully into the room.

Emma's eyebrows rose.

'But of course...I met him at Meriel Faber's divorce party. Meriel was furious when he took me home. She'd got her own eye on him. You'll have to be very careful, darling,' Emma warned Jessica. 'He's frightfully attractive, and very, very sexy...but then, it isn't as though you've fallen madly in love with one another, is it? So clever of Uncle James to offer to make Daniel a partner in the bank. I mean, there's no other way he could ever have achieved that kind of status off his own bat, and with the added promise of his son inheriting the whole lot . . . I promise you that will really put Cousin John's nose out.'

Jessica knew that if she stood there listening to much more she was going to be sick, no longer caring about anything other than the appalling ache burning inside her, the sick shock which had turned her skin clammy and her brain to papier mâché.

'Darling, you look so pale.' As Emma glanced at her watch, Jessica had the feeling that her cousin was secretly laughing at her, as though she knew. But how could she?

'I'm so sorry I can't stay longer, Jess, but I've got a date this evening.' She made a brief kissing noise in Jessica's direction, and pulled on her glove, her smile faintly malicious and triumphant as she paused by the door to say, 'Oh, and one word of warning, darling—don't be silly enough to fall for Daniel, will you? He's a real heartbreaker, or at least he was. I suppose he'll have to reform now that he's about to be a married man. Well, at least you'll be sure of one thing—you're getting a husband who's an excellent lover.' She was almost purring, and Jessica felt her nausea increase.

She waited until she was quite sure that Emma had driven away before staggering upstairs to her bedroom. Once there she crawled into the middle of the bed and lay there, her eyes burning and dry, her stomach still churning nauseously, her mind wrestling with the enormity of her own stupidity.

Daniel had not approached her as a stranger, but as part of a deliberate plan—a plan no doubt set up with her parents' approval, a plan to deceive her in the most cruel and destructive way there was.

And for what? So that her father could have his grandson, and so that Daniel—Daniel whom she had admired, whom she had liked, whom she had loved—could have a partnership in her father's bank.

She closed her eyes, aching to have the power to send herself back to a time before she had known Daniel. How gullible she had been! How stupid! There was no chance that Emma could have made up what she had told her. It had all rung too true. And yet ...

She opened her eyes and stared at the telephone beside her bed.

It would be so easy to pick up the receiver and telephone her mother, ask her—ask her what? If she and her father and Daniel had deliberately deceived her? She started to shake, and curled herself up into a small ball of agonised misery.

What a fool she had made of herself, listening to him, believing him, opening her most private self out to him, loving him, and all the time he had been lying to her, letting her believe that he loved her.

When had he intended to tell her? *After* he had made love to her? she wondered cynically. *After* he had made sure of her, after he was confident enough of her to believe that she would accept his deception? Maybe he wouldn't even have told her until after he had married her—but no, that would have been impossible. He would have had to tell her beforehand... How sure of her he must have been.

Too sure. Much too sure...

Thank heaven she had found out the truth before it was too late.

A small voice mocked her inside, taunting her with the knowledge that it was already too late, but stubbornly she refused to listen to it. She and Daniel had not yet been lovers. She had still not given him that final commitment, and now she never would. Never. Never...

They had arranged to have dinner together, and because her pride demanded it she was determined not to let him see how much learning the truth had hurt her.

So, instead of lying sick and hurting on her bed, she forced herself to go through the motions of preparing for his return as though nothing had happened.

In the small sitting-room, she lit the fire and closed the woven, heavy curtains against the frosty air, switching on the lamps so that the room had an intimate, welcoming warmth.

In the kitchen she set about the preparations for dinner. When she chose she could be an inspired cook, and she chose now, thanking Providence that she had been out this morning and restocked her freezer and cupboards.

Then, when planning the menu, she had thought only of being alone with Daniel, of letting him know subtly how much she had missed him and how much she wanted to be with him. And so she had planned a meal of intimate simplicity. A lovers' meal eaten at a table illuminated only with candles in a room darkened with soft shadows.

She still needed those shadows, but now for a different reason. She had no wish for Daniel to see what she knew lay in her eyes. No wish for him to see how easily he could overrule her pride and her will-power.

No matter what he and her father might have planned, she was not going to be used by them. And to think she had almost wept when he had told her of his teenage dreams—of his supposed realisation that money and power were not the most important things in life. If only she had used her brain then, she might have guessed how deliberately that story had been invented and used. Only someone with a sure knowledge of her personality and her attitudes could have known just how much effect it would have on her. She remembered the way he had listened so sympathetically while she had told him about her past. God, how amused he must have been. Her fingers curled into tight, angry fists. Of course, her father would have told him already about her past, would have cautioned and warned him about what to say and what not to say, and yet, oddly, it wasn't against her father that her hatred and bitterness burned so fiercely.

Her parents loved her. They probably believed they were doing the right thing. They wanted to see her married, drawn back into the ambit of their own lives. Yes, for her father she could find excuses, but for Daniel there were none.

She heard his car long before it stopped outside, marvelling at her senses' ability and unerring instinct to pick out its now familiar sound.

She had deliberately switched off the light in the hallway so that he wouldn't see her face. She was wearing a dress she had found at the back of her wardrobe. A dress her mother had insisted on giving her last Christmas, for the family get-together they always had on Boxing Day.

It was silk velvet, long-sleeved and very fitted, curving to the shape of her body, drawing attention to the narrowness of her hips with its soft silk peplum. The back was slashed open in a deep V to her waist, the peplum had a silk frill that ran down to the hem and a silk bow strategically placed so that it resembled a provocative mock bustle. It was a sensual rather than a sexual dress—a dress that invited a man's touch, that hinted at the secret pleasure of its wearer's body.

It seemed poetic justice that she should be wearing with it the silk stockings which Emma had given her for her birthday, and the high-heeled satin shoes that drew attention to her slender ankles— every bit as slender and delicate as Emma's.

She was even wearing a subtle hint of perfume. She knew that she looked good, but there was no pleasure in the knowledge. Her appearance was a decoy—a means of keeping Daniel's attention occupied, so that when she chose to reveal to Daniel that she knew the truth and that there was no place for him in her life he would find the discovery as painfully shocking as she had found hers this after-noon, albeit for a very different reason.

It wouldn't be Daniel's *feelings* that would be hurt. Men like him didn't *have* feelings. They just had greedy bank accounts.

She let him in and stepped swiftly back into the shadows, not giving him the opportunity to greet her.

Deep inside her a nerve vibrated. If she allowed him to touch her, she would never be able to go through with it. She was still too vulnerable to him to withstand the sheer intensity of her own need.

'Jessica, is everything all right?'

The sharp words were not the ones she had expected. She had thought he would be so trium-phant, so cock-a-hoop with his own success that he would not be able to see beyond the façade she was presenting.

They were in the kitchen now, and mercifully she had her back to him.

'I've missed you,' she told him huskily, and, after all, it wasn't a lie.

It was the wrong thing to say. She felt him walk towards her, bringing the small eddies of cold air from outside. Her spine tensed, the tiny hairs on her skin rising protectively as she willed herself not to turn round, not to do anything other than walk quickly away.

He followed her, stopping her; one hand on her shoulder firmly turned her towards him.

'Something *is* wrong,' he said quietly. 'What is it?'

Could he really tell, or was he simply guessing?

'No,' she lied. 'I was just worried that you might be late . . . the dinner——'

'To hell with the dinner!' Daniel said thickly. 'I've missed you, too.'

The emotion he was projecting caught her off guard. In his absence she had allowed herself to forget what a superb actor he was. She stood still, mesmerised by the fine tremble of his hands as they cupped her face, trembling like a sacrifice on the altar and completely unable to pull herself free. The hard, demanding pressure of his kiss took her by surprise, as did the urgency with which his hands slid over her body.

For a moment she weakened and let herself respond to him, let herself pretend that this afternoon had never happened.

'Oh God, Jess, you don't *know* what you do to me.'

The words muttered against her mouth broke the spell, enabling her to pull herself free of his arms and turn her back on him.

'Dinner's almost ready,' she told him shakily.

He looked at the table and said quietly, 'It looks as though we're celebrating.'

It was her cue, heaven-sent, and it was surely time to bring down the curtain while she still had the strength. She would have liked to drag the finale out until after dinner, to have lulled him into a false sense of security before denouncing him, but she couldn't rely on her own strength of will to last that long.

'We are,' she told him, and then with a composure she was proud of she poured them both a glass of wine and handed him one, saying evenly, 'I'm afraid it's not vintage champagne. My cellar isn't as extensive as my father's,' and then she raised her glass to her mouth and with a brittle smile said shrilly, 'Congratulations on your partnership with my father, Daniel.'

She saw the shock darken his eyes and knew she ought to have been pleased, but instead all she felt was a rolling tide of pain.

She couldn't prolong the farce any longer. What was the point? The very idea of revenge, or hurting him as he had hurt her, was risible.

'It's no use, Daniel,' she told him bleakly, putting her glass down clumsily. 'I know everything. Emma came to see me this afternoon. She told me——'

'Emma?'

'Yes, I know it all now—how you deceived me, lied to me.'

'Jess, let me explain——'

'Explain?' She laughed bitterly. Why had she imagined that, once he realised she knew, he would simply walk away from her in shame? She ought to have realised that men like Daniel didn't know the meaning of the word. Of course he would fight to hold on to what he wanted; of *course* he would use any means at his disposal to persuade and convince her. But she wasn't going to listen.

'Explain what? That it *isn't* true that this morning you and my father were celebrating your joining the bank? Tell me that, Daniel, and then maybe I'll listen to your explanation.'

He looked at her for a long time and then said quietly, 'Yes...it's true your father and I are partners, but——'

'No!' Jessica cut him short. 'Whatever you have to say, Daniel, I don't want to hear it. You've already deceived me once. Lied to me——'

'Lied?'

The anger in his eyes startled her. It wasn't what she had expected. It frightened her and undermined her determination. It wasn't the reaction she had expected. Pleas, excuses, explanations—these she had been ready for, but anger...

'You're everything I most despise in the human race, Daniel,' she told him, rushing quickly into her rehearsed speech. 'Everything I most detest and dislike. There's no place for you in my life, whatever my father might have told you. I won't marry a man who wants me because he sees me as a passport to my father's money—the key to unlock the bank's vaults. The only reason my father is giving you a partnership is because he wants a grandson.' She gave a high-pitched, hysterical laugh. 'But he'd be wasting his money, because there's no way I'd ever let a man like you, a man as contemptible and loathsome as you, make love to me.'

She lifted her hand in a theatrical gesture towards the elegantly set table with its romantic, flickering candlelight and said harshly, 'Yes, we're celebrating. We're celebrating my good fortune in discovering the truth about you before it was too late. You must have been so sure of me, Daniel. So very sure. Telling me you weren't going to rush me. But, you see, you were *too* sure, and now that I know the truth about you——'

'The truth? You know *nothing*!' He slammed down his glass of wine and advanced on her so quickly that there wasn't time for her to move. 'You're so ready to condemn, to criticise...'

He was in a towering, furious rage, and Jessica, who had only seen the gentle, easygoing side of him was transfixed by it.

'...and as for not wanting me—well, let's just see how true that is, shall we?'

She should have guessed, should have known that he wouldn't let her reject him. She hit out at him as he picked her up, but he dodged her blows with ease, laughing savagely under his breath as he carried her towards the stairs.

'So you know everything there is to know, do you?' he taunted. 'Somehow I doubt that, but I promise you this much—by tomorrow morning you will do.'

Shock closed her throat and froze her vocal organs. He couldn't be doing this—couldn't mean what she thought he meant. She had expected that once she denounced him he would leave, but she had underestimated him, and badly, and now for the first time she was frightened.

Frightened not of the raw male anger she had so obviously generated, but of her own leaping response to it. Frightened of the sensations his touch invoked. Frightened of the emotions she had fought all afternoon to subdue.

It wasn't true that she didn't want him. She *ought* not to want him, that was true, but she did, and humiliatingly she suspected he knew it.

Tell him to stop, tell him you've changed your mind—anything... anything to call a halt to what was now happening between them! But, while her feverish brain demanded that she take action, her pride refused to listen. She wasn't going to be the one to back down. She would show him, prove to him that she was stronger than her emotions, stronger even than her love, that she could put both of them aside and lie cold and unresponsive in his arms—that she meant every word of rejection she had thrown at him. Every word.

CHAPTER EIGHT

HER bedroom was in darkness and cold. She had not anticipated being up here with him, and a thin, sharp light from the hunter's moon pierced the curtains in an ethereal shaft.

Unerringly Daniel found his way to her bed, dropping her down on to it and pinning her there.

Her brain shrieked at her to abandon her pride and plead with him to stop this madness and set her free, but the words were locked behind her rigid throat muscles.

Her eyes dared him to do his worst, narrowing like a cornered cat's spitting hatred and disdain.

'I can explain, Jess, if you let me.'

She trembled on the brink of capitulation. What harm would it do? She wouldn't believe what he told her, of course, but it would buy her time, and maybe even...

She caught herself up, knowing her own weakness. If once she let him try to coax her round, if once she allowed herself to believe there might be an explanation...

'Explain.' She gave him a mirthless smile. 'Tell me that Emma was wrong and that my father hasn't made you a partner in the bank. Then I'll let you explain,' she goaded him and saw his mouth grow hard and grim.

'I can't tell you that,' he said crisply.

'Then you can't tell me anything,' she goaded, adding, 'If you rape me, Daniel——'

'Rape?' He drew in a sharp breath, his eyes brilliant with rage. 'Rape you?' She saw the way he fought to control his anger and trembled inwardly. 'Oh, I'm not going to rape you, Jessica, but I promise you this—you'll remember this night for as long as you live, and I promise you the memory of it is going to make you weep endless tears of regret and pain. How dare you deny what you feel for me? How dare you accuse me of something so base——?' He broke off, and her heart leapt. Perhaps after all she had been wrong. Perhaps there was an explanation. But hard on the heels of her joy came reality to bring her crashing back down to earth. Would she never learn? Of course he wanted to make her think, to make her question, to make her doubt . . . and then, once he had done so, he would use that success to build on, to cajole and coax her.

She *must* be strong, resolute. She *mustn't* allow him to sway her judgement.

'Nothing you can say or do will make me change my mind,' she hissed at him. 'Nothing!'

And only realised when she saw the glitter in his eyes the danger of the challenge she had thrown down at him.

'I'm not going to rape you,' he had said, and in her anguish and outrage she had overestimated her own ability to separate herself from her love for him.

Because, despite everything she *had* learned, despite everything she knew, shamingly, there was still love.

She shuddered beneath the force of it as he cupped her face and said harshly against her mouth, so that she felt the vibration of the words against the too sensitive flesh of her lips as well as heard them, 'You won't let me speak to you and explain, but there are other ways of communication. You say you despise me, hate me. I say you're lying, and that you're running away, turning your back on all that we could have shared, just as you turned your back on your parents. You're very good at cutting yourself off from things and people who you no longer want intruding into your life, aren't you, Jess? I can't *stop* you cutting me out of your life, but I intend to make damn sure that you'll never forget me.'

She had never seen him like this before, never guessed he was capable of such emotion, of such terrible, crushing rage. And yet there was no violence in the way his hands shaped her face, no desire to inflict physical pain, and if she hadn't been looking into his eyes and seen for herself the terrible dark bitterness burning there she might almost have felt that he was still the Daniel of yesterday, and that the whole nightmarish interlude with Emma and her revelations were just exactly that— a nightmare.

Listening to him, looking at him, she might almost have supposed that *he* was the injured party, that *she* was the one with the burden of guilt, who had betrayed their love. *Their* love. He had never loved her, never seen her as a woman, merely as the key to power and wealth.

His mouth touched hers lightly, delicately, sensitising the soft flesh of her lips, the tormenting friction making them moisten and cling, her heart and her body sending conflicting messages to her brain.

Where she had expected a roughly brutal attack, a clinical and malely arrogant attempt to force himself on her, she found instead she was being subjected to the subtlest and most undermining form of seduction.

The harder she tried to escape and break free, the more Daniel bound her to him with whispered kisses that caressed her skin and bemused her brain—light, tormenting touches that inflicted pleasure and not pain, and made her long to be free of the restrictions of her clothes so that her flesh could fully experience the tormenting drift of his hands.

'You love me.'

The words seemed to float into her mind, a magic litany that seemed to strengthen the flow of emotion sensitising her flesh.

The words seemed to lure her on, bemusing her mind, promising undreamed-of pleasures, suborning her mind until, sharply and painfully, she remembered the truth and recoiled from him, shivering with self-revulsion.

In the moonlit room he had an advantage which she did not—he could see the expressions chasing one another across her face, the pain and disillusionment, the bewilderment and anguish.

'Jessica, let me explain.'

Lying here, encircled by his arms, his breath warm and moist against her skin, her body sharply hungry for the pleasure it already sensed he could give it, she was tempted to give in, to let him lie and convince her, to let him take them both into a world of fabrication and let's pretend, but stalwartly she knew deep down inside her that the few hours of pleasure which allowing herself to be further deceived would give her would be outweighed a hundredfold by the anguish the memory of that false pleasure would eventually bring.

Summoning up the last of her will-power, she pushed him away and said fiercely, 'No! I already know all I need to know. You lied to me. I asked you if you knew my father. You said no. That was a lie, wasn't it? Wasn't it?'

He was sitting up, looking down at her, one hard hand on her shoulder pinning her to the bed. Why had she ever considered his eyes warm and tender? Now they were as flat and hard as stone, warning her not to press him too hard, but she ignored the warning, driven by demons of her own, by the knowledge that physically he only had to touch her and her body melted, ached, longed...

'You lied to me,' she reiterated. 'Tell me truthfully that Emma is wrong. That you don't know my father. That you've *never* met him. That he hasn't offered you a partnership in the bank.'

He looked at her for a long time, and then said rawly, 'I can't, but...'

She didn't want to hear any more. Stupidly, one tiny part of her had still hoped, had still prayed desperately that by some miracle she might have been wrong. Hating herself for that weakness, she wrenched herself away from him, surprising them both by her sudden surge of physical strength.

She heard the sound of fabric tearing as she moved, and froze, her eyes widening in shock as the shoulder seam of her dress split beneath the pressure of Daniel's grip and the silky velvet fabric slid downwards over her body, revealing first the pale gleam of her collarbone and then, while she stared at Daniel in frozen shock, the soft curve of her breast, her skin robbed of its colour by the moonlight, her throat, shoulder and now fully exposed breast turned to alabaster in its pale gleam.

An odd tension filled the room, a heavy, preternatural silence that seemed to press down on her, making it hard for her to breathe. Her heart started beating erratically. A pulse jumped in her throat and, unable to drag her gaze from Daniel's, she reached up to cover it protectively, only then realising how much of her body was revealed to him.

A fine shudder that had nothing to do with the bedroom's cool air ran through her body; she gulped in air and fumbled for the torn bodice of her dress, but it was too late. Against the chill of her breast she felt the warmth of Daniel's palm. Her pulse-rate rocketed into sharp acceleration.

'Daniel...No...' she denied huskily, but he wasn't listening to her. The air seemed to pulse with the sheer intensity of the emotional vibrations they were each giving off. Desire, anger, pain, and love.

As his hand slid caressingly around her breast, Jessica tried to draw air into her constricted lungs and found that she couldn't. Even before his thumb touched her nipple it was already erect and pulsing with an ache she prayed he couldn't feel. A channel of hot, feverish sensation ran like a cord from her breast to the pit of her stomach, tightening in a sharp spasm of sensation when he touched her, galvanising her flesh like a small electric shock. Instinctively she tensed against it, thus intensifying its power, her eyes turning dark and wild as she forced back the betraying reactionary shudder.

Half-paralysed with tension, she heard Daniel say her name and looked at him, trembling as she recognised the desire glittering in his eyes.

She hadn't bargained for this, hadn't allowed herself to think that a man hard and cold enough to deliberately plan to deceive her in the way Daniel had deceived her might be vulnerable to the overwhelming physical hunger she could see so plainly etched into his face.

He wanted her, and that wanting was real.

She lifted her hand to push him away, but somehow what should have been a gesture of repudiation became a tremulous caress as her fingertips trembled against his jaw and then slid helplessly towards his mouth, touching it as though she were reading braille. Mindlessly she absorbed the messages of this contact between their flesh, her body as still as that of a statue while she traced the fullness of his bottom lip, the clear-cut indentations at the corners of his mouth, the roughness of the skin above his top lip.

She felt him shudder and focused on him, her eyes betraying her bewilderment at her own behaviour. What *was* she doing?

She moved to snatch away her hand, but Daniel moved faster, his fingers closing round her wrist. She curled her fingers into talons, anger striking through her at this imprisonment, but his tongue was tracing spiral patterns against the soft flesh of her palm, ignoring the threat of the nails poised to rake his skin, and she discovered that the silk cord of desire linking her breast to the deepest, most female part of her body extended into other areas of her flesh. Her resistance melted, her body suddenly boneless, formless, pliable and soft, silently inviting him to mould it as he wished.

Without knowing she was doing so, she leaned towards him. His mouth found the pulse beating frantically in her wrist, and her hand touched the deeper, more vulnerable one in her throat, wondering what it would be like to feel his mouth there, claiming the hot pulse of her life's blood as though he knew that he was the one who gave it force.

An odd light-headedness engulfed her. She shivered and pressed herself closer to him, tensing as she felt the abrasive brush of cloth against the tenderness of her exposed breast. The cloth was in her way, a barrier that tormented her tender skin. Impatiently she pulled her hand free and tugged at the buttons on Daniel's shirt.

His skin wasn't like hers, pale and washed to silver by the moonlight. It was warm and golden, his chest deep and broad, silky with the fine dark hair that felt so soft to her fingertips, and yet when he seized hold of her, dragging her almost roughly against him, holding her mouth under his own while he kissed her with a suppressed violence that made her head spin, that same soft hair against her naked breast created such a wanton, delirious sensation within her that she wanted to tear off the rest of her dress and experience that same delicious friction on every centimetre of her skin.

As though her thoughts communicated themselves to him, she felt him reach behind her for the zip on her dress, and quickly strip it from her.

She shivered once as night-cooled air replaced the feverish heat of his body, and then reached towards him, silently and imploringly, beyond reach now of the voices that might have warned her against what she was doing.

As she lifted her hands towards him, Daniel caught hold of both of them, placing a kiss in each palm, and then holding them against his waist where the remaining closed buttons and his belt pressed into her skin.

Kneeling over her in the darkness, he was at once familiar and unfamiliar, and the tension that made her shiver was woman's age-old thrill of excitement-cum-apprehension as she looked into the face of her lover and saw there the uncontrollable quality of his desire, thrilling to it, and yet at the same time apprehensive of it.

And then, as his gaze fastened on her and became absorbed by the beauty of her body, apprehension turned to joy, mingled with a sharp surge of power. He wanted her; this man who was physically so much the stronger and less vulnerable of them both trembled at the sight of her body, his skin flushed with desire, his voice raw with need as he groaned her name, a plea for permission to reach out and touch her.

Blind, deaf and dumb to her own vulnerability, Jessica watched him, glorying in her power, her eyes slanting and narrowed like a hunting cat's, her smile secret and gently taunting. Without knowing what she was doing, she arched her spine, stretching voluptuously, watching him through half-closed eyes, noting the savagely indrawn breath and the hard tension of his muscles. Her hands left his body and one touched her own, hovering over the small triangle of silk that covered the heart of her sexuality. She frowned, her smile vanishing, her eyes clouding as the ache inside her intensified. She looked at Daniel and saw that he was looking back at her. What she saw in his eyes made her pulse leap. He unfastened the remaining buttons on his shirt, pulling it off and unceremoniously dropping it on the floor. The rest of his clothes were equally summarily dispensed with, every action underlined with a fierce urgency that made her heart race. She sat up, watching him, fascinated by the play of light and shadow across his body. When he pulled her against him, moulding her softness into the harder contours of his own body, the shock of the sudden contact with his flesh destroyed the last of her defences. All that she wanted, all that she needed was this—this blissful contact of flesh upon flesh...this heat...this pleasure...this delirium of joy that promised even greater joy beyond its boundaries.

She heard Daniel whispering to her, asking her things that should have shocked her, promising her things that made desire flood through her.

His hands touched her, shaped her, held her, removed from her the barriers of her stockings and briefs, and then shockingly, blissfully, cupped her, stroked her, and finally slid tormentingly against her, where she had ached for them to do, so that all the silver cords of desire running through her body became as taut as an archer's bow, the sensation dragging primitive sounds of pleasure from her throat, while her spine and her body arched and writhed and his mouth moved slowly and mind-destroyingly down the bared arch of her throat, and then further downwards until it rested between her breasts, ignoring their flagrant, thrusting demand to be pleasured by the raw heat of his mouth until she reached out and slid her hands into his hair, cupping the back of his head, feverishly urging him to give her the pleasure the flushed points of her breasts craved.

When he did, it was like nothing she had ever experienced. Her body trembled and convulsed, the shock of the sensations flooding through her betrayed in her eyes. Her body pulsed, ached, yearned towards him so that there was only intense relief in having the hard maleness of him surging against her.

Her breasts, swollen and tender, pushed eagerly against his chest, delighting in the friction of his movements against her, but that sensation, just like that of his hands on her hips, holding her, lifting her, and the sound of his voice, reassuring her, guiding her, were all subordinate to the need growing inside her.

She arched impatiently beneath him, crying out eagerly as his body responded to the invitation of her own and he entered her, offering her a momentary balm to the sharp intensity of her need.

But with each thrust of his body within her own the ache seemed to recede tantalisingly and tormentingly, always just out of reach of the satisfaction his flesh within her own promised.

Her nails raked his flesh, her teeth sharp and demanding, her body wild with need and inciting a similar savagery within his so that suddenly his movements were no longer controlled and tender, but fierce and elemental, like the eternal, relentless pounding of the sea against the land, driving her closer and closer to that place where the ache could no longer be controlled.

The climax came so quickly and was so earth-shatteringly powerful that it awed and half terrified her. She had a momentary glimpse of Daniel's face, his control shattered; he cried out something to her, his voice harsh and unfamiliar. She had a swift and terrifying awareness of reality and all that went with it, and then her body slid over the edge into darkness, carrying her mind with it.

She slept heavily and dreamlessly, awoken by the sound of her alarm. Her body felt unfamiliar and alien, voluptuously lazy, and yet at the same time sharply alive. In the harsh morning sun her skin seemed to possess a new luminescence, as though it glowed still with remembered pleasure. She turned her head and realised that she was alone as the memories came flooding back. There was a folded note propped up against her radio alarm with her name written on it.

She reached for it, opening it, her hands trembling.

'We *have* to talk. Daniel.'

We have to talk—and she knew about what. How he must be gloating! How he would enjoy ruthlessly reminding her of all that her foolish body had betrayed. He had found the way to entrap her now, and he wouldn't hesitate to use it again. She had no faith in her mind's ability to withstand the desires of her body any longer. Panic engulfed her. She had to escape, to get away...

And then she remembered that in a few days' time she was due in Northumberland. Jane wouldn't mind if she arrived earlier than planned. Daniel wouldn't be able to find her there. Neither would her parents. From that sanctuary, she would write to her parents and tell them that nothing on this earth would induce her to marry Daniel. That she would rather cut herself off from them completely than allow him to so much as lay a finger on her ever again.

She shuddered, clutching the bedclothes to her nude body, remembering how eagerly, how wantonly she had sought far more than the brief touch of his hands on her body last night. Far more. Well, now she had to pay for that weakness, that madness.

All the time she was making the preparations for her flight, her mind was punishing her with vivid mental flashes of tormenting memories of the past twenty-four hours, providing them in taunting mixtures of contrast: her anger and determination to eject Daniel from her life after she had learned the truth, side by side with her wanton, eager pleading for his lovemaking—images that made her stomach churn nauseously and her skin burn with hot, bitter misery.

She had no excuse to offer herself, no explanation nor reason; she had wanted him to make love to her, had eagerly and willingly aided and abetted him in her own mental humiliation.

With good reason had he laughed at her when she'd accused him of threatening her with rape.

Her hands shook as she packed the few clothes she would need; her mind wandered as she tried to concentrate on the far more important tools she might need.

Half of her resented her own weakness, in stealing away in fear, in not confronting Daniel and her parents and making her parents see what they were doing to her.

Her father wanted her married to Daniel, and had bribed him into agreeing, but she doubted that her father had realised just what methods Daniel would use to get her to consent to that marriage. She doubted that either her mother or her father realised how Daniel had damaged her, destroyed her. How he had tricked her into trusting him— into *loving* him.

The nausea rose up inside her again and she fought it down, hurrying through her preparations with a hunted, frantic tension that drove her until she was at last in her car and on her way north.

She was leaving without any letters, any explanations. She would write to her parents from Northumberland. And as for Daniel . . . She smiled mirthlessly and bitterly.

She had no doubt that once he discovered her flight he would realise how pointless it would be for him to pursue this charade of having some believable explanation for his behaviour. How could there be any kind of explanation? He had already admitted he couldn't deny that her father had offered him a partnership, and that he had accepted it. He was condemned by his own mouth.

Driven by the relentless pain of her own self-betrayal, she made good time to Northumberland, not stopping to break her journey other than when she had to refill her car with petrol.

The thought of food nauseated her. Her body was drawn tight with tension and revulsion—revulsion against herself, against her weakness, against that small pocket of rebellion deep inside her which said that her traitorous flesh wanted Daniel as its lover.

Symond Court was several miles away from its nearest village; a gaunt stone edifice that stood with its back to the North Sea and guarded from its vantage-point the empty countryside that surrounded it.

It was a house that had known many changes of fortune. Built originally by one of the Percies, it had passed out of their hands during a game of dice in the eighteenth century.

The man who won it had married a girl twenty years his junior on the strength of its possession, and her family, having discovered that, while he might own the house, he owned no wealth to support and maintain it, punished him for his deception by encouraging his wife into an affair with a prominent Minister of State.

The child of that affair was the only child of the marriage, and in due course he inherited Symond, but preferred not to live there, associating its bleakness with his own childhood.

In Victorian times it had seen a revival of its fortunes and had been sold to one of the new breed of monied men thrown up by the development of the railways. He had shrewdly married his eldest son to a daughter of the Percies, thus establishing for him a social respectability he himself could never attain. The house remained in the hands of their descendants until after the end of the First World War when, crippled by death duties, and having seen the deaths of his father, uncles, brothers and cousins, the sixteen-year-old who inherited it informed his trustees that he wanted it sold. For him the place would always carry too many memories of weeping women, of death and pain; he wanted to escape to somewhere where there was warmth and laughter. The land was sold off to various tenant farmers, the house and a handful of acres gradually falling into disrepair as the trustees sought unsuccessfully for a buyer.

The National Trust had taken it over thirty years previously. It wasn't a great house, nor a particularly famous one, but it did faithfully mirror the changes undergone by many English country houses in the centuries since it was built in 1690 to the present day.

The tapestries had been found hidden away in one of the attics, and after a good deal of research it had been established that they had originally been designed for the state bedroom, and that their designs had originated from Daniel Marot, Huguenot architect, who had been such a great favourite with William of Orange and his Queen Mary.

Jessica had been both thrilled and saddened the first time she saw the tapestries: thrilled by their beauty and rarity, saddened by their neglect and the signs of wear and tear. She had discussed then with Jane the work that would be necessary to restore and repair them.

At any other time the challenge of being invited to undertake this work would have delighted her, but during her long drive north it had been her present-day Daniel who had filled her mind to the exclusion of everything else, and not the Daniel Marot whose skill had originally designed the tapestries.

When she'd stopped to fill her car with petrol, she had taken the precaution of telephoning Jane to alert her to her early arrival.

'No problem,' Jane had told her warmly. 'In fact, I'll be glad of your company. The caretaker and his wife are away on holiday at the moment and the house is closed to visitors, so it's rather lonely.'

It had started to rain as she left the motorway, and now low grey clouds hung over the house, adding to its outward grimness.

The drive, bare of its avenue of once elegant limes, looked stark and uninviting, and Jessica shivered a little as she looked at the grim façade, aching for the warmth and security of her own home, for Daniel's arms...

She shuddered tensely, slamming her hand hard against the steering-wheel, hating herself for her own weakness. She had to forget him, to put him out of her mind, to stop thinking about him.

Jane was waiting for her as she drove round to the rear of the house and parked her car.

'Are you all right?' she asked in some concern as she helped her remove her luggage from the car.

Jessica gave her a tight smile, wondering what it was that had given her away, until they were inside the house and a quick glance in a mirror showed her her white, strained face, and huge dark eyes. The skin beneath them was taut and discoloured as though bruised. She looked, she admitted to herself, haunted.

'It's a long drive,' she said obliquely in response to Jane's question.

'Well, you've certainly made good time. I wasn't expecting you for another couple of hours at least. Let's have a cup of tea, shall we, and then I'll take you up to the tapestries. We've moved them into the workroom in the stable block. The light's much better in there. I'm afraid you're going to be cold, though. We daren't risk turning on the central heating. They're so fragile and brittle in places.'

The tea she made was hot and strong, with an aromatic, almost bitter taste. It scalded Jessica's throat, bringing her back to life. Watching her tremble suddenly, her face flooding with colour, Jane said quietly, 'I don't want to pry, but if you do want to talk...' She pulled a wry face. 'If it's man trouble, I've been there myself...more than once.'

Jessica smiled bitterly. 'Is it really so obvious?'

Jane grimaced apologetically.

'Well, yes, I'm afraid it is.'

Much as she liked her, Jessica couldn't talk to her. The hurt was still too raw, too new. All she really wanted to do was to crawl away somewhere and die, but she couldn't do that. She had to get over it, to go on...

She looked out of the window at the darkening sky and said, 'I think it might be a good idea for me to leave the tapestries until tomorrow. The light just isn't good enough now.'

'OK. I'll take you up to your room.' Jane hesitated and looked at her. 'I'm afraid I've got a date tonight, but I could cancel it if——'

Jessica shook her head. 'No, please don't—not on my account. I'm not very good company at the moment and, to be honest, I'd rather be alone.'

Jane gave her an understanding smile. 'Well, there's food in the fridge, and plenty of canned stuff in the cupboards. Just help yourself, and then tomorrow after breakfast I'll take you across to the workrooms.'

In normal circumstances the room Jane showed her to would have enchanted and delighted her; as it was, she barely noticed the rich damask of the hangings enclosing the bed, only half listening to her as Jane described how the pattern had been copied from a faded, torn scrap of fabric found during the renovation work.

'We had it copied in Lyons, using the traditional methods of weaving the fabric, and using modern dyes. Because the traditional dyes were so unreliable and faded so easily, we tend to forget how very rich and striking their original colours must have been—not to say garish,' Jane added with a grin, reaching out and touching the bed hangings, admitting, 'I love this shade of red, though. It's so vibrant and warm.'

The room had a fireplace, but, as Jane explained to her, no fire could be lit in it. 'Fire hazard,' she added pulling a face. 'We simply daren't take the risk.' She hovered for a moment, and then said awkwardly, 'Look, if you want some company, I could always cancel my date.'

It was only pride that enabled Jessica to lift her head and force a smile to her own lips.

'No. It's all right. I might *look* suicidal,' she said, striving to make her voice light and succeeding only in giving it a metallic brittleness, 'but I promise you I'm not.'

Not suicidal maybe, she acknowledged after she had reassured Jane and closed the door after her, but desperately aware of an inner aloneness, a coldness of spirit that pierced her, reminding her too painfully of how only a short time ago she had known the deep inner warmth that comes from close intimacy with one special person.

She thought she had known all there was to know about pain and loneliness, but she was beginning to discover she had not. When she had turned her back on her parents and the life they had planned for her, she had suffered, missed them, but that pain was nothing like the pain that rent her now.

Her body ached for sleep, just as much as her mind ached for release into oblivion, but both were denied her as she moved restlessly in the huge tester bed, her mind racked by self-contempt and anguish, her body racked with its longing to have Daniel beside her. Holding her, touching her, loving her...

With a low moan she turned on to her stomach, burying her face in her pillow. This was sheer stupidity, idiocy. If she allowed her thoughts to continue unchecked they would surely drive her to madness.

Cravenly, she longed for some magic pill which would miraculously wipe her heart and body clear of any memory of Daniel, but no such cure existed.

CHAPTER NINE

WORKING on the tapestries might be keeping her hands busy, but it was doing nothing to control the waywardness of her thoughts, Jessica acknowledged, lifting her head from her work and gazing unseeingly through the large north-facing window of the workshop.

She had been in Northumberland for two days, trying to concentrate all her energies on the task confronting her, but it wasn't working. Physically she might be here in Northumberland, but mentally, emotionally, she was still trapped in her bedroom at home, aching for Daniel, wanting him, loving him.

Her work was almost completed. Soon it would be time for her to return home. Jane had a busy social life and had invited her to join her this evening, when she was going out to dinner with friends.

Jessica had refused. She preferred to be on her own. There was no point in inflicting her misery on others.

Already it was mid-afternoon. Soon it would be dusk, and too dark for her to work. The evening stretched out in front of her emptily.

The house had a library full of books, and the small sitting-room Jane had invited her to use had a television set, but nothing held a strong enough appeal to wrench her mind away from its obsessive dwelling on Daniel.

She considered going to bed early, but the thought of going there, going compulsively over and over every second she had spent with Daniel, everything they had said and done, and then contrasting the rosy dream she had allowed herself to be drawn into then with the harsh reality of the truth, held no appeal either.

There had not been a moment from the time when she had last seen him when she had not been thinking about him. She had come up here to escape, to give herself a breathing space, but what if once she returned Daniel was not prepared to accept that she no longer wanted to see him? He was a determined man.

She was just watching the late evening news when she heard a car outside. She got up and went to the window, but it was too dark for her to see anything. It was still too early for Jane to be returning, and a tiny tendril of apprehension feathered down her spine. What if someone was about to break into the house? It contained many valuable pieces of furniture and paintings. And then the enormous, old-fashioned and very loud doorbell rang demandingly, and she dismissed her fears as idiotic and hurried downstairs.

It took her several minutes to deal with the complicated locks and bolts on the door, but foolishly, as she opened the door itself, she forgot to secure the safety-chain. She wasn't used to living with such elaborate security precautions, and it was only when the door was pushed open abruptly from the other side and Daniel strode in that she realised her own folly.

Stunned by the unexpectedness of his arrival, here where she had believed he would never know where to find her, she could only stare at him in stupefaction.

'Surprise, surprise!' he mocked her as he pushed the door closed with a gentle, and yet somehow rather intimidating, movement of his hand. He smiled at her equally gently, and she shivered, hating herself for her weakness.

That feeling which had invaded the pit of her stomach when she opened the door and saw him had nothing to do with hatred or anger.

It had been instinctive, automatic, indelible. She still loved him.

Shaken by her own stupidity, she turned away from him, thinking in some way that she might be able to remain stronger if she wasn't looking at him, if she was not being subjected to his effect on three of her five senses all at the same time; and the other two, touch and taste... She shuddered visibly, recalling all too clearly just how his body had felt beneath her touch, just how his skin had tasted...

'What are you doing here?' she demanded abruptly. 'How did you find me?'

She wasn't going to look at him, but the hair on the nape of her neck lifted gently in warning as he moved towards her and she felt the air behind her stir.

She froze, willing her body to repudiate him if he touched her. But he didn't, and only she knew just how much her recalcitrant body ached to feel the warmth of his hands on it.

'If you want to vanish completely, you shouldn't leave names and addresses on your answering machine,' he told her calmly.

Of course—that message from Jane. How could she have been so idiotic? And then shamingly she picked up on the cynicism in his voice, and whirled round, denying hotly. 'If you think I did that deliberately, so that you would come running after me...' Pain and anger choked her. 'You had no right to go into my house, to pry into my private things.' He was looking at her grimly, like an adult waiting for a child to finish a temper tantrum; his very lack of response to her accusations lashed her into a greater fury. 'You really are desperate, aren't you? I suppose it was naïve of me to think that once you'd discovered that neither lying to me nor seducing me were going to work, you'd give up.'

He was still watching her silently, distantly. Out of the corner of her eye she caught sight of her handbag, and, picking it up with an impulsive, bitter movement, she fumbled inside it and extracted a handful of silver, throwing it at his feet and crying fiercely, 'Thirty pieces of silver. That's the usual payment for a Judas, isn't——'

And then stood frozen with shock and horror at her own uncontrolled behaviour while he slowly picked up the money, and then said softly—too softly, her mind warned her—'You miscalculated. There are only twenty-nine pieces here, which means that I still haven't had full payment.'

He took one step towards her, and then another, and too late she saw how deceptive his distant calm had been. In reality he was far from calm; the lack of light in the hallway had not allowed her to see the hard glitter of anger-spiked bitterness in his eyes, nor to guess at the tension of his body beneath his seemingly relaxed pose.

He was going to touch her, kiss her, and once he did—once he did, no matter that that kiss was given in punishment and rage, she would be lost, as lost as she had been when they'd made love, clinging to him, crying to him to do with her what he wished, to make of her what he willed.

'What is it?' she cried out frantically, betraying more of her terror than she knew. 'What do you want?'

But she already knew what he wanted. He wanted her father's wealth, and ultimately her father's power. He wanted the bank, and to get it he was prepared to fulfil the conditions her father had set upon its acquisition. Marriage to her.

'Don't touch me,' she begged wildly, her self-control shattering under the tension of his slow advance towards her. She had already backed as far away from him as she could, and her skin burned as she heard her own shaming plea and recognised the panic and fear in her voice.

'Touch you?' He stopped and frowned, his mouth curling as though in disgust at the very thought, his expression suddenly changing as the rage died out of his eyes, the hot red glitter replaced by cold hardness. 'I haven't come to play games, Jessica. I'm not here on my own behalf, but on your mother's. Your father's had a heart attack. He's in Intensive Care. You mother needs you with her.'

She didn't believe it. He was lying to her—using another ploy to weaken her.

'You're lying to me,' she whispered, her face suddenly ashen. 'I don't believe you.'

'No, you wouldn't, would you?' He reached for her too quickly for her to avoid him, grasping her arm and dragging her towards the telephone on the table by the stairs.

Holding her arm in a grip so tight that she could already feel her flesh going numb, his eyes never leaving her face, he punched out a number into the telephone.

Jessica heard it ringing, and then when the ringing stopped he said tersely into the receiver, 'Intensive Care, Sister Allen, please.'

Jessica's head started to thud uncomfortably. What if he *wasn't* lying? What if it *was* true? What if her father's heart attack had in part been brought on by the discovery that she was refusing to fall in with his plans?

Anger, fear, pain...a conflicting mix of emotions gripped her as she stood there, her throat dry with apprehension, her eyes locked on Daniel's.

Holding the receiver slightly away from his ear, so that she could hear the voice on the other end, he said tersely, 'Sister Allen, I'm sorry to bother you. It's Daniel Hayward. How is Mr Collingwood?'

There was a moment's pause, and then Jessica heard a woman's voice saying quietly, 'Rather poorly at the moment, I'm afraid, Mr Haywood. As you know, he's had a major heart attack, and I'm afraid it's still far too early to give you any more information than that.'

Jessica stared at the receiver. She tried to speak, and found that her tongue had become thick and clumsy and that her head was buzzing. She saw Daniel put down the receiver and then turn to look at her, a frown replacing the grim hauteur with which he had been regarding her.

'Oh, God, don't look at me like that, Jess,' she thought she heard him saying, but the words were indistinct and fuzzy, and the world was turning dark all around her. She was being sucked down into a dark, cold vacuum, which she fought desperately against letting claim her.

Sick and dizzy, she was conscious of Daniel picking her up and depositing her in one of the hard antique chairs that furnished the hallway.

She wanted to close her eyes to blot out his face, but she knew that if she did she would lose consciousness completely. She had to focus on something to will herself not to give way to the panic and fear inside her.

'I'm sorry, I shouldn't have broken it to you like that.'

Compassion. Concern. She stared blankly at Daniel, her body trembling as though she were frozen. He was holding her hands, she suddenly realised, crouching down on the floor beside her, his thumbs registering the too rapid race of the pulse in her wrists.

'Let go of me, I'm all right.'

Her father in Intensive Care... Strange how she had never thought of her parents as vulnerable before. Strange how she suddenly felt as frightened and abandoned as a small child. She hadn't lived with them for years—rarely saw them—and if asked would have said that she was an adult and no longer dependent on them in any kind of way, but now she realised that it wasn't true.

She struggled to stand up, swaying uncertainly on her feet, her eyes blank.

'I must go home. My mother. Why didn't *she* ring me?' she cried out in sharp anguish.

Daniel was still holding her hands, still refusing to let her go.

'Perhaps she was afraid you'd refuse to come,' he told her quietly.

'Refuse?' She looked at him, her eyes dark with shock. 'but he's my father.'

'Yes, but you've made it very plain that you want to keep your life separate from theirs, haven't you, Jessica?'

'Because I couldn't be what they wanted. But that doesn't mean that I don't *love* them, that I don't *care*...'

She started to cry, her body shaking with emotion as she fought to control her feelings.

'I must go home. My things... I need to pack.'

'I'll do that for you,' Daniel told her. 'You just tell me how to find your room, and then we'll be on our way—at this time of night we should make good time.'

'We?' Jessica stared at him, and then said shakily, 'I'm not going back with *you*.'

The look he gave her made her feel small and ashamed, as though somehow she was behaving more like a child than a woman.

'I have my own car here,' she pointed out in a calmer voice. Naturally I——'

'Naturally nothing,' Daniel overruled her. 'You're in no fit state to drive, and if you're honest you'll admit it.' He saw her face and smiled unkindly.

'Yes, I know how much against the grain it must go that I'm the one to have had to break the news and witness your... distress. You've had a severe shock, Jessica, and if you won't consider the risk to your own life of driving several hundred miles while suffering from that shock, then at least think of the lives of the other people you might be putting at risk.'

She looked away from him, unable to deny the truth of what he was saying.

'Besides,' he added calmly, 'my car will make much better time than yours.'

'But you must be tired yourself,' she pointed out. 'You've only just arrived.'

Suddenly she realised how much he had taken on his shoulders, how very different his behaviour was from what she would have expected, but then she reminded herself of all that he stood to lose if anything should happen to her father, and of what a golden opportunity this must be to him to try to bring her round, to persuade her...

She ought to make a stand, to tell him that there was no way she was going to allow him to drive her back to London, but the thought of the long, tiring drive south, the knowledge that she was in no fit state to make that drive, silenced her.

'Your room?' Daniel demanded curtly.

Numbly Jessica told him, too drained to continue arguing. She watched with listless eyes as he went upstairs, and then, remembering his long drive and the equally long one ahead of them, she roused herself and went into the small kitchen which formed part of the caretaker's suite of rooms.

Jane had told her to make herself completely at home in this part of the house, and she knew the other girl would not mind her raiding the fridge in order to make some sandwiches and a flask of coffee for the homeward journey once she knew what had happened.

Thinking of Jane reminded Jessica that she ought to leave the other girl a note. She was just writing it when Daniel walked into the kitchen with her case.

'I've made you some sandwiches,' she told him curtly. 'I thought you might be hungry.'

She saw the surprise lighten his eyes and felt a momentary pang of remorse, a longing for things to be different, and even a rebellious wish that she had never opened the door to her cousin—never learned the truth.

'Something wrong?' Daniel asked her, watching her closely.

Hot colour scorched her skin. How he would laugh if he could read her thoughts.

In addition to filling a flask with fresh coffee, she'd poured them both a mug. She knew *she* needed the reviving, caffeine-induced surge of energy the drink would give, and she suspected that, although he wasn't showing it, Daniel must be feeling the effect of his long drive.

Turning away from him so that he couldn't see her face, she picked up one of the mugs and handed it to him, saying shortly, 'No, of course not.' And then suddenly, as though in denial of her claim, her hand started shaking, slopping the coffee on to the table, and to her horror she felt her eyes filling up with tears as a mixture of fear and urgency swept over her. Hating herself for being so vulnerable, she added bitterly, 'After all, it's not as though I've any reason to feel shocked and upset, is it?'

He gave her a cynical look. 'If you're trying to tell me those tears are for your father...'

His jibe stung and she retaliated bitterly. 'Just because I won't allow my father to run my life for me, it doesn't mean I don't love him... that I don't care... He *is* my father.'

'Is he? I had the impression your relationship with your parents was something you preferred to pretend didn't exist.'

His accusation hurt her, leaving her bereft of any defences, and too vulnerable to the small inner voice that told her that there must have been many times in the past when she had unwittingly hurt her parents, more so than she herself had ever realised, if it were true that her mother had felt so unsure of her response that she hadn't wanted to telephone her with the news of her father's heart attack. She had to remind herself that even now he was not above using her vulnerability to reinforce his own position, to emotionally coerce her.

'I never said that,' she denied sharply.

'Not in so many words, but you certainly gave me that impression. You don't trust anyone who knows your parents—hardly the sentiments of a loving child,' he taunted her.

'Maybe not, but they were certainly justified, weren't they?' Jessica accused, anger overtaking vulnerability. 'I may not share my parents' views on the direction I want my life to take, but that doesn't mean I don't care.'

There was a small silence, and then Daniel said grimly, 'Tell that to your father if——' He broke off, but she knew what he had been about to say. 'If he's still alive.'

Something broke apart inside her, spilling pain throughout her body, unleashing a veritable Pandora's box of emotions so complex and agonising that she wanted to cry out in protest against them.

'I can't be the daughter my parents want,' she said huskily, speaking her pain out loud. 'I *can't* sacrifice my life and emotions to the bank.'

Daniel had finished his coffee.

'Time to go,' he told her curtly, cutting across her emotional outburst.

It was only later, sitting next to him in his car as he drove south, that she remembered that he had never given her back the money she had thrown at him in such anguish and disdain, and for some reason she couldn't quite analyse that struck a tiny note of alarm somewhere deep inside her.

They were on the motorway, which was mercifully free of heavy traffic at this time of night, and Daniel had been silent for so long that it was a shock to hear him saying smoothly, 'I take it the bedroom you were in wasn't very warm.'

Astonishment made her turn her head to look at him, her expression unguarded and puzzled as she looked at his unreadable profile. He was concentrating on the road, not looking at her, even though she knew he must be conscious of her scrutiny. A car came up behind them, being driven far too fast, and he changed gear, pulling to one side to allow it to pass. The movement caught her attention, causing her to focus automatically on his thigh.

A huge wave of sensation washed through her, her body quivering as her mind fought against the images flashing across her brain. It shocked her that such a small, mundane movement could have the power to arouse images of such sensuality and intimacy, and her mind recoiled, horrified by what the conscious part of it considered to be an unforgivable invasion into the privacy of another person.

She had never before in all her life looked at a man and immediately conjured up a mental vision of him naked, aroused by desire, offering the pleasures of his body to her for her enjoyment. And what was even more disturbing was her own reaction to the wantonness of that imagery.

Confused and ashamed, she forced herself to drag her gaze from his body and focus on his face, her mind swimming with shock and bewilderment.

'My bedroom, cold?' she managed to stammer. 'I... No... I don't... What makes you think that?'

'The nightdress you were wearing,' he told her casually, momentarily and totally unexpectedly diverting his attention from the road to her.

'My nightdress?' She frowned, remembering how quickly she had packed for her journey north, wrenching out of a drawer a hideous winceyette nightdress which she had been given as a Christmas present one year, and by Emma, of all people.

She felt herself go hot and then cold as she realised that if Daniel had found her nightdress, then he had doubtless found and packed her underwear as well, although why she should feel so embarrassed at the thought of him touching her things she really had no idea. If she was honest with herself, anyway, it wasn't the thought of him touching the clothes he had removed from her drawer that disturbed her so much, but the remembered sensation of his hands removing them from her body.

'Yes ... yes, it was cold. The house doesn't have central heating...' She realised too late that she was babbling a panic-stricken explanation and fell silent, not sure which of them she hated the most, herself or him.

'You realise that we still have to talk, don't you?' he continued calmly.

'Talk?' She jerked herself back to reality and gave him a bitter look. 'What about? You can't have anything to say that I want to hear.'

'No,' he agreed acidly. '*You* wouldn't. All you want to do is run away, to punish me the way you punished your parents.'

Jessica sucked in her breath, outraged that he should dare to accuse her.

'I thought you were a woman,' he went on inexorably, 'but you're not. You're a spoiled, selfish child who isn't capable of thinking beyond her own immaturity——'

'You're just saying that because you still think you can persuade me, convince me,' she interrupted him hotly, only to fall silent as he said coldly,

'No, Jessica. I have no intention of persuading or convincing you of anything. I was foolish enough once to offer you an explanation—an explanation of something that ought to have been taken on trust,' he told her grimly. 'But you *have* no trust. You couldn't wait to believe the worst of me, could you? You couldn't wait to reject me. Oh, no. I'm not your doting daddy. I'm not going to pander to you, coaxing and persuading you. Trust, love— they're two-way things, and if you think I want to share my life with a woman who doesn't respect me enough as a human being to know that I wouldn't deceive her without some very good reason——' He broke off and looked directly at her, and Jessica felt her heart plummet, and a horrid feeling of shame and misery engulf her. There was no love in his eyes, no warmth, no teasing, male appreciation, only a flat, metallic hardness that repudiated her and denied her, and for some reason she felt as though *she* were the one in the wrong.

'I don't know why you're telling me this,' she said fiercely. 'There's no relationship between us any more.'

'At least that's something we can agree on,' he countered coldly. 'All I'm doing is making my position clear. I'm here on your parents' behalf, not my own, so please disabuse yourself of any idea you might have that I'm going to try to coax or persuade you in any shape or form.'

'I'm glad!' Jessica snapped. 'Because it wouldn't work. We've both already agreed, it's finished.'

'Not quite,' Daniel told her silkily.

A tiny *frisson* of fear feathered down her spine. There was something in the way he spoke, something in the cold, hard way he smiled at her...

'There's still the matter of your twenty-nine pieces of silver. Poor Jessica,' he mocked cruelly. 'You couldn't even get that right, could you? One day, not very far from now, you're going to wish more than you've wished anything else in your life that you hadn't made that gesture, Jess.'

'Never,' she told him quickly. 'Never!' And then wondered uncertainly why it was that she was having such a strong premonition of danger.

It must have something to do with the power of his voice, she comforted herself, because there was absolutely no way he could be doing anything other than making the most outrageously impossible threats... Was there?

CHAPTER TEN

DESPITE Jessica's insistence that he take her straight to the hospital, Daniel took her instead to a small and very obviously expensive private hotel, where he stunned her by announcing that he had booked her a room.

'What for?' she demanded.

'Your mother will be at the hospital with your father. I suggest that it would be wiser to telephone and discover how your father is before rushing round there.'

While she could see the wisdom of this, Jessica felt compelled to point out that she could quite easily have gone to her parents' home in Kensington rather than come here with him.

'Do you have a key to the Kensington house?' he asked her quietly.

Jessica's face flamed. She didn't, of course.

'Your mother has enough to cope with without worrying about you. I told her I'd bring you to London and that I'd make sure you had a bed for the night.'

'Very sure of yourself, weren't you?' Jessica stormed at him. 'I suppose what you had in mind was my sharing *your* bed.'

She was stunned by the look of acid disdain he gave her. It silenced her, leaving her throat dry and her muscles tense.

'Now who's guilty of coercion?' he asked her softly, watching the colour rise up under her skin and then saying cruelly, 'If you want to make love with me, why not be honest and just say so?'

'I don't,' Jessica told him wildly, her heart pounding with shame and rage. 'And anyway, it wouldn't be making love—it would be just sex.'

She felt her heart plummet as he looked at her, his mouth twisting.

'You almost tempt me, but I don't have the time or the inclination to play those kind of games. There's a telephone here in the foyer. I suggest we ring the hospital from there, just so that neither of us gets any confusing ideas about each other's motives. I *was* going to offer to take you up to your room, but under the circumstances...'

Jessica had never felt so humiliated in her life, and the worst thing of all was that his accusation held a grim kernel of truth, even if she had only realised that fact herself after he had pointed it out to her.

As he walked across to the public telephone Jessica wished she had the strength to dismiss him and tell him that she didn't need his help, that she would make the call, but she knew that some part of her was frightened—frightened of what she might hear, frightened of the pain of learning that her father was dead, frightened of the burden of guilt that news would bring—and so, torn between resentment and anguish, she watched while he dialled the number and spoke once more to the ward sister.

The conversation was brief, and she was unable to hear it without joining him in the cramped intimacy of the booth—something she had no desire to do. Another weakness, another failing, she taunted herself bitterly as she waited for him to rejoin her, her stomach in knots of tension, her mind clouded by fears.

'He's holding his own,' he told her tersely. 'He's only allowed one visitor at the moment, and it's your mother's wish to stay with him.'

'Does she know? Does she know I'm here?' she asked him unevenly.

'Yes. I told her you were here. The best thing you can do now is to try and get some sleep,' he told her, turning his back on her, dismissing her, she recognised.

She swallowed and said painfully, 'If anything should happen to my father...'

'I've asked the hospital to let us know.'

She felt perilously close to tears, and ached for the warmth of his arms round her, holding her, protecting her...

What was she thinking? There was no safety, no warmth, no protection for her in Daniel's arms.

She went up to her room alone. It was well appointed, and a good size. Someone had already taken up her case, and there was also a thermos of coffee and a plate of delicate sandwiches, the sight and smell of which made her stomach lurch protestingly with nausea.

She spent what was left of the night tormenting herself with regrets for all that she had left unsaid and undone to show her parents how much she did love them.

Daniel had made her see the different and hurtful construction someone else might have put on the way she had so determinedly detached herself from her parents' lives—not knowing that it was because of her great fear that out of love for them she might commit herself to a life which she had known would ultimately lead to intense unhappiness for her.

Had she been as selfish and thoughtless as Daniel had implied? Perhaps she *could* have explained in more depth to her parents just why she had felt too vulnerable, too fearful of succumbing to the need she had felt in both of them, but more especially in her father, that she should be a part of the chain that linked the past with the future.

Only now, alone with the bleakness of her thoughts, did she realise that part of her fear, her resentment, had sprung from jealousy of the tradition which had made the bank such an important part of her father's life; as though, in turning her back on it, she was making a childish attempt to demand from him a statement that *she* was more important than the bank, like a child jealous of its siblings.

A flush of shame for her own immaturity stung her skin. Nothing would make her change her mind about the necessity for her to live her own life. She could never have made a career in the bank and found the contentment and satisfaction she found in her present work, but she could have explained in more depth, discussed, talked to her parents about her feelings, instead of seizing the excuse of her kidnap and thus foisting on them both, but more especially on her father, a burden of guilt that it was their fault that she had left the bank, that it was the bank raid and her subsequent ordeal at the hands of her kidnappers which had led to her desire to change her whole way of life, when in truth that had simply been an excuse she had seized upon because she was too weak to admit the truth.

Dawn came and brought no surcease from her mental anguish. Her head ached; she felt sick, alternately hot and cold as she tried not to let her imagination portray her father's death.

As her feeling of nausea grew she put her hand on her stomach and prayed grimly that the only reason for her nausea was her fear for her father. To have conceived Daniel's child would be the ultimate irony—her father would have his grandson, after all, or maybe a granddaughter, and she... She gave a fierce shudder and banked down hard on her too fertile imagination. Didn't she already have enough to worry about?

The discreet tap on her door startled her. For a moment she thought it might be Daniel, and the fierce thrust of emotion that speared her at that thought was its own betrayal, and didn't need underlining by the swift downward plunge of disappointment when the door opened and a smiling girl came in carrying a tray of tea.

Thanking her, Jessica poured herself a cup, her hand shaking when she recognised the aromatic blend she herself favoured first thing in the morning. Only Daniel could have ordered that particular tea for her, and to her consternation her hand wavered and her eyes filled with tears. When he had already hurt her in so many harsher ways, why it should be this small, deliberate hurting that should cause her to waver on the edge of breaking down, she did not know.

She looked at the phone. How long before she could ring the hospital? On impulse she picked up her clothes and hurried into the bathroom, showering and dressing before she had time to change her mind, leaving the cold tea undrunk as she found her handbag and let herself out of the room.

The hotel foyer was deserted apart from the receptionist on duty, as well it might be at this early hour.

Outside, the sun was struggling to emerge from behind a barrier of clouds, the air sharp and bitter, flavoured with the scents of the winter to come.

The commissionaire found her a taxi, and as it traversed the still quiet city streets Jessica realised with a shock how close it was to Christmas.

The knowledge brought a sharp stab of urgency, a need to see her father. Memories of past Christmases when she was a child flashed through her mind. How loved she had been, indulged but never spoilt. She closed her eyes in mental agony, wondering why it had taken Daniel to show her all she had deliberately blinded herself to.

Outside the hospital she hesitated, half yearning to turn back, afraid to go forward, afraid of the pain that might be waiting for her, and then a smiling porter asked her helpfully if she was lost, and she told him she was looking for the intensive care unit.

After he had directed her to it, he added warningly, 'Not that they're likely to let you in—not unless...' but Jessica was already hurrying away, suddenly in a fever of urgency to see her mother.

The doors to the intensive care ward were firmly closed. A nurse was seated outside at a desk, working on what looked like a horrendous mass of paper. She looked up curiously as Jessica approached her.

Awkwardly, Jessica gave her name, her tongue suddenly clumsy, her heart beating too fast with nervous dread.

'My father——' she began, and then broke off as the ward doors opened and her mother approached.

She hadn't seen Jessica, and the shock of seeing her normally immaculately groomed and coiffeured mother without her make-up, her face drawn, her hair untidy, traces of tears clearly discernible on her face seemed to seize her body in a paralysis of dread, and then her mother saw her and opened her arms to her, saying tremulously, 'Darling, it's all right. Your father is doing very well. He's over the worst now, and there's every chance that he's going to make a full recovery.' She gave a rather watery chuckle. 'His doctor says that this attack was a warning shot across the bows, and that if he takes heed of it . . .' She hugged Jessica tightly. 'Come in and see him for yourself.'

Shakily Jessica followed her into the ward, tensing at the sight of her father wired up to what seemed to be a formidable array of machinery, but he had seen her, and he was smiling at her, and suddenly she was overwhelmed with such a flood of love and awareness that it was impossible for her to speak.

'So Daniel found you,' her father said gently. 'He said he would.'

Daniel . . . The sound of his name brought her crashing back to earth, but she couldn't, wouldn't, do anything to spoil this moment, so she smiled and held tight to her mother's hand while the three of them shared the intensely emotional communion with one another.

Later, euphoric with relief, she went back to the Kensington house with her mother, surprised to discover how hungry she was, how suddenly alive and aware.

'I thought Daniel was going to come to the hospital with you,' her mother remarked as she made some coffee.

'I didn't want to disturb him,' Jessica fibbed. In truth she hadn't wanted Daniel to accompany her, and the note she had left him had been brittly polite and cold.

'No, he must have been exhausted,' her mother commented. 'I can't tell you how marvellous he's been. It's such a relief to know that the bank's in such capable hands. I can't help thinking that it's the stress and strain of these last few months which have contributed to your father's heart attack. The fear of the bank being taken over by some huge conglomerate whose ideology is totally different from your father's...I know that when Daniel first approached him with his company's offer, your father adamantly refused to consider it.' She chuckled reminiscently. 'He was furious when he came home. Outraged at this up-and-coming entrepreneur who dared to believe he could take over. And then, when he'd calmed down, he admitted to me that there were problems with the bank, that some of the shareholders might be tempted into selling their shares to one of those corporations that specialise in dawn raids on people whom they see as their competitors, followed by a rapid take-over of the company and then its destruction. Daniel at least, he admitted, wanted to maintain the bank as a going concern, to improve and enlarge its business activities, but his pride was stung a little, I think, by the knowledge that such a young man had built up a company large enough to take over the bank.' She smiled warmly at Jessica. 'That's something you and your father have always shared. Your pride.'

Jessica stared numbly at her.

'Mother, are you trying to tell me that Daniel has *taken over* the bank?'

Her mother looked puzzled.

'Well, yes, dear. I thought you knew that. Of course, there hasn't been an official announcement as yet. After all, your father and Daniel only signed the formal agreement a few days ago. Actually your father was rather cross.' She pulled a face. 'Of all the things to happen, your cousin Emma arrived in his office just as the formal signing was taking place. She had apparently ignored his secretary's request that she wait until your father had time to see her. Your father wasn't very pleased, I'm afraid, especially when his secretary told him that she found Emma actually eavesdropping outside his office door.'

The kitchen had started to spin dizzily around her. Jessica clutched the edge of the table, feeling she had stepped into a horrific nightmare.

'But I thought... I thought that Daniel was joining the bank as a junior partner.'

She saw her mother frown.

'Oh, no. What on earth gave you that idea?'

Jessica couldn't speak, and her mother mused maternally, 'We were so pleased when we learned that Daniel had bought a house so close to your village. I'm afraid, between us, your father and I must have bored him to tears singing your praises, but we're both so proud of you and all that you've achieved.' She bit her lip and added a little uncomfortably, 'Don't be cross with me, darling, but I'm afraid I did rather overdo the maternal bit a little in suggesting he might care to get in touch with you, but your father and I both liked him so much. I think it must be the eternal curse on all mothers that, where their children are concerned, they just can't resist matchmaking. I think he was rather uncomfortable about my suggestion, but obviously he did take me up on it.'

Her head whirling slowly and cautiously, Jessica began to question her mother, and what she learned made her tremble inwardly with sickening recognition of her own folly.

It was Emma who had lied to her, not Daniel. There could be no doubt about that, but, just to make doubly sure, she said as casually as she could, 'Emma called to see me a few days ago. She seems to know Daniel quite well.'

Her mother pulled a face. 'Well, that's another small problem we've had. Daniel was here for dinner one night when Emma arrived unexpectedly. She said she knew Daniel, and I asked her to join us, and I'm afraid I put him in a very embarrassing position. It turns out, although I suspect he's given us a rather sanitised version of the story, that Emma was introduced to him at a party some time ago, and that since then she's been making rather a nuisance of herself. He was quite blunt about it, and told us that he doubted that her feelings were in any way involved, and that it had been obvious to him from the moment he was introduced to her that she was, as he put it, on the look-out for a wealthy husband.'

Her mother spread her hands. 'What could I say? We all know that it's true. Of course, I apologised for putting him in an embarrassing position, but since then I'm afraid your cousin has been virtually hounding him. Your poor father was furious that she took advantage of her relationship with him to turn up at his office like that, and it was obvious she knew Daniel was there. I'm afraid he had to speak rather severely to her, and I also think that it was his interview with her that was at least partly to blame for his heart attack.'

She gave a faint sigh. 'I'm afraid there are people in this world who, like your cousin, can never be content with their lives, and so must always be searching for something more. I feel very sorry for her. Now tell me, darling—what do you think of Daniel?' she invited eagerly.

Jessica gave her a wan smile, her face totally devoid of colour. 'I'm sorry, Mum, but I'm not feeling very well... I...' She stood up unsteadily and raced for the downstairs cloakroom.

'It's just the shock of everything,' she muttered feebly once she was back in the kitchen with her mother fussing anxiously over her. She wasn't lying, after all—just not explaining exactly what kind of shock it was she was enduring.

'You must be exhausted,' her mother sympathised. 'I ought to be myself, but I think the relief

of knowing your father is going to be all right has
put me on some kind of elevated plateau.'

'I think it's called euphoria,' Jessica teased her
weakly. Oh, how she wanted to be alone—needed
to be alone—but she owed it to her mother to stay
here with her. For once in her life, it was time to
put someone else's feelings before her own. She was
here to *help* her mother, not to burden her.

Later she was thankful for the constantly ringing
telephone, for the people who had to be advised of
her father's progress, for the hundred and one small
jobs her mother found her to do, because they kept
her physically occupied, kept her from being left
on her own to dwell on the enormity of her mis-
judgement of Daniel.

'I can explain,' he had said, but she wouldn't let
him, and now it was too late. She remembered the
money she had thrown at him, the words she had
said . . .

For three days she managed to keep up a pretence
of normality, but on the third morning she answered
the telephone and, on hearing Daniel's voice on the
other end of the line, started to tremble so violently
that she dropped the receiver and then fled to her
room.

She wasn't surprised when her mother followed
her there and said quietly, 'Do you want to talk
about it?'

Surprisingly, she discovered that she did, grateful
for the fact that her mother listened in silence, not
interrupting until she had finished.

'Oh, Jessica,' she said sadly.

'Yes, I know,' Jessica whispered hollowly. 'He'll never forgive me. How could he? I've destroyed...what...whatever there might have been. But why didn't he tell me?'

Her mother was watching her pityingly, and she hadn't even told her the very worst of it—that shameful, irrational gesture of high drama that was now rebounding on her so cruelly.

'Perhaps he tried,' her mother said tentatively. Jessica started to deny it, and then remembered that there had been an occasion on which Daniel had seemed on the verge of saying something to her. And then, of course, afterwards, he had tried to explain, but she had refused to let him. 'If he still loves you——' her mother continued, but Jessica made a gesture of dismissal and said bitterly,

'Why not say, if I had loved him? I did...I do:...but love on its own isn't enough, is it? I mistrusted him. I believed Emma without stopping to question what she was telling me. I refused to give him the benefit of the doubt, to listen when he asked me to. How much contact is Daddy likely to have with him, once...once he's back on his feet?' she asked obliquely.

Her mother sighed. 'Well, the plan is that Daniel will take over as chairman, but he has asked your father to stay on in an advisory capacity, and, of course, your father will retain his seat on the board. I'm afraid there will be rather a lot of occasions when he's likely to be a part of our lives. Of course, you no longer live here——'

She broke off, remembering just how close to Daniel Jessica did live, and it was left to Jessica to say quietly, 'Yes, well, in the circumstances, I'm sure it would be the best thing all round if I found somewhere else to live.'

There was a sad silence, and then her mother offered, 'Perhaps if your father or I were to explain?' But Jessica shook her head firmly.

'No. No more running. No more evasion. No more not facing up to the truth. I've learned that much, at least. No, there's only one thing I can do—must do.' She bit her lip and asked quietly, 'Do you . . . do you have a telephone number where he can be reached?'

Her mother frowned. 'Yes, I think so. It should be in your father's diary.'

It was, but the efficient secretary Jessica spoke to could offer her no other information than to say that her boss was unobtainable and taking a few days' leave of absence.

That left her with only one option.

She wasn't going to deceive herself. There was no going back, no remote chance of undoing the wrong she had done him, but at least she could apologise, admit her error, make it easier for her parents in their business involved with Daniel and make it clear to him that, whatever her private feelings, she was not, like her cousin, going to make a nuisance of herself. In fact, she was going to make sure that after she had delivered her apology—paid her debt, so to speak—there would be no chance of their paths ever crossing again. If they didn't she might, somehow, find the strength to go on living without him, but if she was subjected to the torment of seeing him . . . Her body shuddered with pain, her face deathly white.

Her mother willingly agreed to lend her her car when Jessica explained what she had to do, although she expressed concern about her physical health.

Jessica gave her a wan smile. 'I have to do it, Ma,' she told her. 'Please don't try to dissuade me.' She pulled a wry face and admitted shakily, 'If you did, I'm afraid I'm all too likely to succumb, and if I did that ...'

Her voice tailed away, and she saw from the sympathetic way her mother was looking at her that she understood how important it was to her pride and self-respect that she admitted her error to Daniel—not because she entertained any foolish idea that he would forgive her, not even because she wanted to be forgiven, but because her own self-respect demanded that she do so.

It was going to be hard enough to build a life for herself without Daniel in it. It would be even harder if she also had to live with the knowledge that she had once again run away, found excuses for herself, refused to face up to her own responsibility for her own life.

She knew that Daniel wasn't still staying at the hotel to which he had taken her when he had brought her back from Northumberland. She knew he wasn't in his office. But that did not necessarily mean that she would find him at Little Parvham.

Nevertheless, she drove there, parking her mother's car outside the Bell and forcing herself to walk into the bar and ask the landlady if she knew where Daniel was.

The landlady of the Bell was a voluble, cheerful woman who enjoyed talking. After she had questioned Jessica about her own recovery from the shock of being in the post office when the would-be robber walked in, she informed her that Daniel was, to the best of her knowledge, out at his house.

Thanking her, Jessica made her way back to her car, battling against a cowardly impulse to find some reason for delaying the moment when she would have to face him and admit how she had misjudged him...when she would have to apologise to him and beg his pardon for the inexcusable insults she had thrown at him.

It was probably just as well that the road was empty of any other traffic, because her concentration was certainly far from exclusively focused on her driving.

She was shaking inwardly with tension and nausea when she eventually turned into the drive. There was no sign of Daniel's car when she haphazardly parked her own, but, assuming he had parked it to the rear of the property, she walked in through the open front door, hesitantly calling his name.

The silence of the dilapidated building was vaguely unnerving, but Jessica forced herself to walk into the middle of the hall, knowing that in reality her tension was not caused by the house, but by her own reluctance to see Daniel.

When her tentative call brought no response, she walked slowly upstairs.

What must have once been a very attractive gallery ran around three sides of the hallway, so that from below it was possible to look up to the roof and admire the ornate plasterwork of the domed ceiling above her, but where there must once have been an ornamental balustrade surrounding the gallery there were now yawning gaps, and as she reached the landing and glanced back down into the hallway below Jessica had a sickening sensation of giddiness. She had never liked heights, but, oddly, when she had been round the house with Daniel she hadn't been aware of the potential danger of the unguarded landing, and, frowning a little, she felt sure that when they had come round there had been some sort of protective rail running round the gallery at waist height.

If there had, it was now gone, and, keeping well back from the edge, she called Daniel's name again.

Silence... Frowning, she pushed open one of the bedroom doors and went to look down out of the window at the rear of the house. There was no sign of Daniel's car. He wasn't here.

Not sure whether it was relief or disappointment that was her sharpest feeling, she turned on her heel and walked out of the bedroom, closing the door behind her.

The floorboards on the gallery were uneven and warped—rotten in places, she recognised, frowning as she noticed the betraying signs of damp and decay when she really studied the floor.

Still frowning, she suddenly remembered that Daniel had not shown her this side of the gallery, explaining that the floorboards were in a very dangerously advanced state of decay, and that one of his complaints against his original builder had been the fact that he had removed the supporting beams from the hallway below without taking the trouble to shore up the floor with the appropriate props.

As she remembered Daniel's warning, Jessica moved forward quickly—too quickly, she realised, gasping with shock as the floor beneath her suddenly gave way, causing her to lose her footing and fall heavily.

The sensation of the floor falling away beneath her was one of the most terrifying she had ever experienced. She clung desperately to it as it tilted and then dissolved around her, crying out sharply in shock.

'Jessica! Don't move. Lie still.'

Daniel was here. She drew a shaky sob of relief and opened her eyes, quickly closing them again when she saw how much of the floor had given way beneath her, and how very precarious the one remaining strut was that supported her.

'Jess... Are you all right? Have you broken anything?'

Daniel was standing at the top of the stairs, his face unexpectedly strained, only yards away from her, but between where she was clinging to her strut and where he stood in safety was a yawning, empty gap where the floor had once been.

'Jess!'

She tried to concentrate. Her fall had winded her, her arm ached, but she was sure nothing was broken.

She started to shake her head, stopping when Daniel called out quickly, 'No, don't move—not yet...' but it was already too late. Jessica heard the ominous creak, felt the deathly ripple of movement that warned her that the joist couldn't support her for much longer. She looked down at the floor so far below her, and wished sickly that she hadn't, all too easily picturing what would happen to her vulnerable body if it plummeted on to it. Below her, the wreckage of the first fall had thrown up sharp spears of broken wood, and she shuddered, imagining them piercing her flesh, her organs...

'Jessica, listen to me. You can't stay there, the joist isn't strong enough. I'm going to lie down here and reach out to you. I want you to wriggle as far forward as you can.'

Jessica measured the distance between them in disbelief—no matter how much both of them stretched out, they couldn't bridge it.

'No,' she whispered croakily. 'No, it's too much of a risk.'

'All of life is a risk. Trust me, Jess. Trust me. I promise I won't let you fall.'

Trust me... All of a sudden hot, salty tears began to flood her eyes. What had she got to lose? If she fell, if she died...what was her life anyway, without him?

'Watch me, Jess,' he told her quietly. 'Watch me, and I'll tell you when.'

Her throat had gone dry and sore. Painfully she watched as he lay down on the floor and stretched out towards her.

'What I want you to do is to wriggle as far forward as you can, and then when I say jump...'

He couldn't mean it! But he did... 'Trust me,' he had said, but why should he put his own life at risk to save hers? Why should he give her so much when she had given him so little?

'Now, Jess...Now!'

Fear thrilled through her, but his command couldn't be ignored. She edged as far forward as she could, fighting to ignore the dreadful slow swaying of her precarious perch.

'Now...jump! Jump!'

Closing her eyes, she levered herself off her small platform. The sensation of falling...was sickening... She opened her eyes just as Daniel grabbed hold of her, hauling her unceremoniously on to the landing beside him.

The relief of it affected them both.

'What the hell were you doing up there?' Daniel demanded roughly, almost shaking her, while the tears poured down her face and she stammered huskily,

'I came to apologise. You weren't here...and...I fell.' She gave a deep shudder, and suddenly realised that he had stopped shaking her, but that he was still holding her. She tried to move away from him and immediately his hold tightened.

'Oh, no, you don't. Why did you *want* to apologise?'

So he was determined to extract his pound of flesh. Well, she could scarcely blame him.

All her carefully prepared speeches had gone completely out of her mind. She looked at him, and whispered huskily, 'Ma told me...about you taking over the bank. I realised Emma had lied to me. I just don't know what to say.'

She bit her lip and turned her head.

There was silence, and then he said softly, 'You could always try telling me that you love me.'

Her head snapped round, her eyes widening with anguish. 'Please, don't,' she begged, thinking he was deliberately taunting her. 'I know it's what I deserve, but I don't think I can...' and then to her horror fresh tears started to fall.

'Say it!' he insisted.

Through her pain she stared at him, and knew there was no escape.

'I love you.'

Again there was silence, and then he told her quietly, 'And I love you, too.'

'Don't,' she whispered brokenly, unable to bear the pain of his mockery.

'Don't what?' he mocked her, but his voice was rough and slightly unsteady. The way he was looking at her transfixed her, flooding her with a shock of hope.

'What is it you don't want me to do, Jess? Don't love you? Don't ache for you? Don't need you? Tell me *how* I can stop. Oh God, Jessica!'

And then he was kissing her, urgently, desperately almost, and her senses, starved of the intimacy of him, flooded her with their tumultuous response to him. She clung to him, kissing him back, opening herself to him, murmuring soft words of longing deep in her throat.

When he eventually released her, half laughing and half crying, she said the only thing that seemed to matter.

'Daniel, I love you so much. Can you forgive me? I was so wrong, so stupid...'

'We both made mistakes,' he told her gently. 'When I walked into the hall and saw you clinging to that joist, realised your danger... If I'd thought your lack of trust in me had killed my love—if I'd thought that, well, I very quickly realised how wrong I was, and I knew then that I'd rather go through that rejection a hundred times than see you die. And besides, it wasn't entirely your fault ... I *could* have made you listen, explained. I *should* have told you earlier that I knew your father, but after what you said about not trusting people who knew your parents...' He gave a brief shrug. 'I was already committed ... knew I loved you. I told myself I'd tell you the truth once I'd won your trust——'

'Mother told me everything,' Jessica interpolated. 'I should never have listened to Emma.'

'And I should have realised what a vindictive little soul she is, and been a little more careful in telling her that there was no place for her in my life and that I loved you. I should have realised she'd try to make trouble between us, especially after she gatecrashed my meeting with your father and over-heard me telling him I was worried about the fact that I hadn't been able to tell you about my take-over of the bank, and that I didn't want my take-over as chairman officially announced until I'd had a chance to tell you about it. I was going to tell you that evening ... had been screwing up my courage to tell you——'

'That money I threw at you,' Jessica interrupted unhappily. 'That was awful of me. There isn't any excuse. I was so unhappy.'

'Mmm ... and you still owe me one piece,' he teased her, adding thoughtfully, 'Maybe you should give me a kiss instead.'

'Suppose I were to buy back the other twenty-nine pieces from you?' Jessica suggested instead.

He pretended to consider it. 'At what rate?'

'Mmm... A thousand per cent—one kiss at a thousand per cent for each of the twenty-nine pieces.'

'Twenty-nine thousand kisses? I don't know... how about twenty-nine thousand nights spent in my arms instead?' he murmured. 'Twenty-nine thousand... of course, you'd have to marry me. Now that I'm the chairman of such a respectable institution as Collingwood's I have my reputation to consider, you realise.'

'Twenty-nine thousand nights?' Jessica pretended to consider.

'In my arms,' he reminded her. 'Of course, if you're not sure you could meet such a long commitment, I could always...'

He was kissing her throat as he spoke, the words muffled against her skin.

'You could always what?' Jessica prompted huskily, trying to ignore this blatant seduction.

'I could always find some way of making the terms more acceptable.'

'In what way?'

He was still kissing her, his teeth nibbling provocatively at her vulnerable flesh, making her quiver outwardly as well as inwardly. 'Perhaps a small demonstration.' His hands were shaping her body, and she made a soft yearning sound deep in her throat, her fingers curling round his wrist, holding his hand against her breast while she moved her lips eagerly along his jaw, seeking his mouth.

'Never again,' he told her rawly, meeting the eager pressure of her kiss, 'never again are we going to let anything come between us.'

'Never,' Jessica answered. 'Never!'

Coming soon to an easy chair near you.

FIRST CLASS is Harlequin's armchair travel plan for the incurably romantic. You'll visit a different dreamy destination every month from January through December without ever packing a bag. No jet lag, no expensive air fares and *no* lost luggage. Just First Class Harlequin Romance reading, featuring exotic settings from Tasmania to Thailand, from Egypt to Australia, and more.

FIRST CLASS romantic excursions guaranteed! Start your world tour in January. Look for the special **FIRST CLASS** destination on selected Harlequin Romance titles—there's a new one every month.

NEXT DESTINATION:
AUSTRALIA

 Harlequin Books

JTR3

Harlequin American Romance

You'll flip . . . your pages won't!
Read paperbacks *hands-free* with

Book Mate · I

The perfect "mate" for all your romance paperbacks

Traveling • Vacationing • At Work • In Bed • Studying
• Cooking • Eating

Perfect size for all standard paperbacks, this wonderful invention makes reading a pure pleasure! Ingenious design holds paperback books OPEN and FLAT so even wind can't ruffle pages – leaves your hands free to do other things. Reinforced, wipe-clean vinyl-covered holder flexes to let you turn pages without undoing the strap . . . supports paperbacks so well, they have the strength of hardcovers!

Pages turn WITHOUT opening the strap

SEE-THROUGH STRAP

Reinforced back stays flat

Built in bookmark

BOOK MARK

BACK COVER HOLDING STRIP

10˝ x 7¼˝ . opened.
Snaps closed for easy carrying, too